THE EMPTY CITY

BERIT ELLINGSEN

The Empty City
Copyright © 2011 by Berit Ellingsen
All rights reserved

August 2011 edition
ISBN 978-8299873604
Jnana Press

http://emptycitynovel.com
http://beritellingsen.com

"The Crabs" was first published in SPLIT Quarterly no. 2, April 2011.

"Vindication" was first published as part of "Repatriation" in The Subterranean Journal no. 1, April 2011.

Cover photography by Michele Pandini and Wandeclayt M.
Cover design by Tom Brierley.
Editing by Toni Rakestraw.

Part 1: Presence

Part 2: Giving In

1: Early Summer

The apartment building was nineteen stories tall with six identical faces, each presenting three rows of balconies with gleaming glass railing. It was one of five towers constructed on reclaimed marshland north of the city. The area had been too wet for development, but modern draining and construction techniques made the towers possible, creating much needed living space for the city. To make the overpriced apartments more attractive, a train line was built to the towers.

Every day the trains transported the young and successful and the not so young and less successful that belonged to the five buildings.

Brandon Minamoto left the train station and started on the path to the honeycomb towers. The glare from the bright light and the steel surfaces of the station faded in the evening darkness. The serpentine footpath was lit by white, swan-necked lamps. Nocturnal insects flew up from the moist grass and into the artificial light. The sound from the motorway and the city was a distant song in the humid air.

He drew in the scent of mowed lawn in the park, exhaust fumes from the motorway and rotten water from the surrounding marsh. What a quiet and beautiful night! His body was soft and pliant, even his shoulders and neck, after a long day at work.

Steps of dark granite led up to glass doors framed in polished steel. The front and sides of the foyer were all glass. The granite in the stairs continued on the floor inside. The building admitted him with a sigh.

The foyer was empty. He only saw people there during rush hour in the morning. Then his neighbors looked faint and distant, as if they weren't real. The recessed lights in the ceiling illuminated the foyer with a golden light. All four elevator doors were open, their call panels shining green. Next to the elevators, a wide staircase led up into the building. He disliked the greedy gape of the stairs and turned away as he passed it. He entered the far left elevator and pressed button number eighteen.

The elevator opened to a long hallway in the east corner of the building. The floor had a burgundy carpet patterned with white and gold. The walls were as red as the carpet. White glass funnels cast a bright light into the ceiling and down onto the floor. He followed the hallway north. Behind the deep red walls, bodies were sleeping, dreaming. He found that knowledge very uncomfortable. His own bed stood along the outer wall instead of the corridor.

Last fall he had crossed the mountain massif north of the city on foot. It had felt like the stone and the sky cared about him. The sun warmed his back and the stiff mountain grass whispered when he waded through it, as if it knew he was there and appreciated his presence. He missed that kindness and awareness from the walls at home. But the dead glass and concrete couldn't afford what he wanted, so he remained disgusted by the bodies that dreamed too close.

2: The Extremist

He removed the keycard from his wallet and pushed the plastic rectangle into the slot in the door. The lock clicked open. Before pressing the handle down, he peered into the peephole to see what the apartment looked like without him.

Through the small lens he could just make out the illumination from the spotlights over the kitchen counter. The north wall of the apartment was a large window with a sliding door that lead out to the balcony, with an expansive view of the marsh and the residential areas. But like the black hole at the center of the galaxy, the peephole compressed everything to a small space that even light had trouble escaping. When that thought passed his mind, he smiled.

He entered his black hole apartment and closed and locked the door. Sometimes he dreamed that the door was too small for the frame, preventing him from securing the barrier, despite his repeated attempts to lock it. Those dreams made him wake up sweating. He stepped onto the brown hand-woven rug he had bought for the small entrance. Following the habit of his childhood home, he untied his shoes and placed them under the coat rack. Then he hung his suit jacket up.

The warm darkness inside the apartment felt as pleasant as the night outside. It was quiet. The cats must be asleep on the bed. He loosened his tie and went to the bathroom to wash the city off his hands. The iridescent blue, brown and golden tiles in the bath reflected the faint light from the hallway. The multi-colored shimmer made the room seem larger than it was.

The sink was a smooth bowl of brown and green acrylic, layered to resemble natural ceramics. Its blended earth colors and gentle slope reminded him of handmade bowls from his father's country. It conformed to his idea of worn and gentle elegance, his reason for choosing the expensive item. But he'd never admit that to his father, or anyone else.

When he was done, he dried his hands on the smallest towel on the heating rack. The thick fabric whispered in the silence. In the mirror he was a tall, lean shadow. He pushed his long bangs away from his forehead. He didn't feel like going through the routines, so cardio it was instead. He pulled the large towel from the heating rack and left.

These last months he had wanted extremism, needed to see how far he could take himself. How long could he work? How long could he go without food? Without

5

sleep? How far could he run? He isolated himself because it took time to work that much, run that long, lose that much sleep. None of his friends wanted to join in on the experiment. But to him, a pattern of increasing physical and mental challenges was familiar, even comforting. And when he had exhausted himself enough, he slept, for what felt like days; like Endymion, the eternal sleeper. Overdoing was his panacea for boredom.

"You're going to hurt yourself," his brother Katsuhiro said, when he told him about the new project.

"Explore with me, then," his cousin Beanie said. "I know a few unsafe places under ground. Should be a nice exercise to get into and out of."

"Sure," he said, smirking.

"What's the point and what the hell is wrong with you?" Michael said.

"Everything, baby, everything," he replied.

He locked himself into the empty space of the gym and pool on the top floor. All inhabitants in the tower had access to the fitness room for a small monthly fee, much more reasonable than membership in the sports clubs in the city. He had made good use of it. Saving was one thing he couldn't overdo. Most of his income went to pay for the apartment. But he comforted himself with an adage from his father's country: "A warrior will feign wealth even when starving." Funny how mom's country didn't have sayings like that.

Under the glass and steel ceiling the twenty-five meter long pool was a gently moving surface with a panoramic view of the marsh. In the distance the motorway ramps curved in on themselves, and the bog glittered faintly in the light from the city.

He stripped and ran to the pool. With the light off it felt like rushing towards the edge of the roof. He imagined the cascade of metal and glass shards that would happen if he crashed through the wall. Instead, he turned and dove into the cold water.

3: The Primary World

The shallow end was two meters deep. The dive took him along the teal blue tiles at the bottom. He kept his body straight but relaxed, to get as much distance from the momentum as possible. When he slowed down, he made one arm stroke and flattened his arms against his side, just like he had learned in special training. Midway in the pool, the floor sloped to four and a half meters, and the water turned ocean dark. He did one breast stroke and kept his arms out, ready for the next arm stroke. That brought him to the end. There, he turned sideways and pushed hard away from the tiles.

Two more cycles of unhurried arm and breast strokes took him back to the shallow side. His eyes and lungs and arms and legs burned, but he hadn't had enough. He turned and started on the third length. He focused on the calm water, and the depth of the night sky that watched him through the ceiling. His throat caught a few times as he swallowed for air, but without drawing water in. Finally, he reached the pool wall, broke the surface and breathed.

Stars gleamed overhead. He relaxed and floated on his back. The ripples splashed languidly against the edges of the pool, then fell quiet. One person couldn't disturb the large body of water much. He turned his head from side to side to watch the sky with the light-sensitive edges of his eyes. He could see the fat spine of stars going down the middle of the firmament, the center of the galaxy, the winter street.

The sight reminded him of a story he had read, about a man who was stranded on an alien ocean planet. The planet was sentient but benign. After a while, the man realized that the planet was aware of him and kept him alive. In the end, the protagonist let the planet turn him into one of its own sea creatures, so he could live there forever.

He continued, swam seventy-five laps on the surface till he was sore and panting. Then he floated for a long time beneath the stars. When he was calm after the work-out, he drew a deep breath, dove down to the bottom of the pool and watched the stars through the night-filled water. He grew tired and closed his eyes.

He saw the tower and the region as it had been a hundred thousand years ago. The land was an uninterrupted swamp, with generous vegetation and drooping deciduous trees. A shallow river from the mountains brought fresh water into the wide outlet.

In the warm water long-legged fowl, birds of prey, cayman crocodiles and snakes hunted. The green surface hid fish, amphibians, crustaceans and insects. The swamp teemed with life that ate itself and was reborn into a new shape every second. The air was hot and smelled of humidity, rotting plants and decay. A thin mist filled the delta. The sun was a pink disc in the sky that illuminated the still waters and the waiting trees with a gentle, white light.

4: The Third Rail

The phone rang. No, the sound had no ring tone so it must be the door. Who could it be so early?

"Don't tell me you forgot our date!"

Beanie's voice on the door phone sounded crackly and thick. He was standing by the door, but smelled of sleep, so he must have come from bed.

"Just a moment," he muttered and pressed the button on the door phone.

Beanie (real name Beatrice) walked into the entrance. She was petite, twenty-four, Michael's younger sister and a friend since early childhood. She knew the city better than he did.

"Did I wake you?" Beanie said, grinning at him. He was dressed in nothing but his underpants. He covered his eyes with his hand.

"What time is it?" It felt like he had been asleep for days.

"Fifteen thirty-nine," Beanie said. "On Saturday." Her eyes gleamed.

He smirked. "Ow, thanks." He threw her a vitamin C pill from the bowl by the mirror.

Beanie caught it with her mouth.

"Where are we going?" he said, already knowing the answer.

"Down below," Beanie said. "Where the dead men roam!"

He laughed and headed for the bedroom and his clothes. The battery on the camera was flat. He had forgotten to recharge it since the last trip.

They rode the elevator down to the garage, stood under the bright light and the LED stars in the ceiling. He glanced down at Beanie. She looked at him.

"Are you scared?" he said.

"Of course not," Beanie grinned.

They fell in silence. The elevator doors opened to gasoline-scented air.

He backed out of the parking spot, brought the car up the ramp and out of the garage. A thin mist obscured the marsh, the cemetery and the city, transformed the sun into a pink disc.

"What a weird sky," Beanie said.

"Do you like it?" he said.

Beanie nodded. "It looks strange, but beautiful. I like it."

He smiled. They sat in silent togetherness for the rest of the drive, while the landscape flew by. It was four in the afternoon, but the sun sat high above the horizon.

Beanie led him to one of the train stations in the city. It was Saturday afternoon and no rush hour, but the platforms were crowded. They rode the escalator down.

"Are you sure this is the right stop?" he said, taking in the people above and below them. So many heads in different colors; black, brown, red, purple, sandy, blond, gray.

Beanie grinned. "Of course I'm sure. It's a secret place."

She took him down to the westernmost platform on the lowest level. The space was filled with professionals on their way home from work, young mothers bringing their strollers home after a day in the city, teenagers going out, an old couple with a bouquet of flowers, young immigrants that spoke loudly in a foreign tongue. The curved walls of the station wore glazed blue and white tiles that made him think of dinner porcelain. His mother's butcher had the same tiles in his shop.

At the back of the platform sat a low wire fence with a sign that said: "Employees only. Keep out!" Beanie vaulted over the thigh-high barrier. He glanced at the crowd on the platform. No one seemed to be paying them attention, and he couldn't see any security guards either. He swung himself over the fence, kept one hand on the metal to dampen any rattling. Around the corner of the platform was a white metal door with a long latch. Beanie looked down the tracks. If a train arrived at the station, the passengers in the rear cars would see them. She quickly pulled the latch on the door down and the metal creaked open.

"Get in," Beanie said.

He ducked into the darkness. Beanie followed and shut the door behind her. She lit a small head flashlight and placed it in her short, brown hair.

"Here." She handed him a narrow, black cylinder.

"Thanks." He clicked on the soft end and a bluish-white beam emitted from the torch. "Nice. Got more batteries if we run out?"

"Always," Beanie said, patting the side of her jacket.

They followed the platform to the end. A staircase led down into darkness.

"Have you been here before?" he said.

Beanie chuckled. "Never, but it's supposed to be safe. As long as we don't meet any trains." He hoped she was joking about the "never" part.

"You're trying to scare me," he said.

Beanie grinned.

The stairs had the same white and blue tiles as the platforms above. Each step was edged with a strip of metal for traction. The brass colored metal had once been criss-crossed but was worn smooth. The stairs sagged in the middle and slanted downward. In the warm darkness he could hear booms, bangs, chatter, laughter and screams.

They followed the stairs down. There, another platform was waiting. When they stepped onto the planks, the structure creaked loudly and dust plumed up. At the end were more stairs. Beanie jumped down on the first step.

"Are you coming?" she said. Her eyes gleamed.

They descended together. The gloom was hot and seemed impenetrable. The sounds from above faded. There was nothing but darkness and tunnels and stone. The stairs ended in another wooden platform.

"We have reached the bottom of things!" Beanie announced.

So she had been there before, he concluded, and cheered with her.

"This old thing might not be safe," he said and tapped his boot on the dry wood. He moved to the gravel below the platform. The dry pebbles creaked.

"Don't step on the third rail now," Beanie grinned. In the beam from the flashlight her teeth shone white. Beads of sweat were visible on her forehead and on the freckled bridge of her nose.

The tubular walls carried thick bundles of cables, covered in black dust. The wires pointed into the darkness. The air was stale and tasted of iron and asbestos. His heart beat slowly and heavily, weighed down by the stone and the warm darkness. But he could still see the sun above them. It had moved a fraction towards the horizon, and the sky was as white as before.

Beanie chewed on her lip, but whether it was from excitement or fear, he couldn't tell.

"Come on, let's follow the tracks," she said. "There are no trains going this deep any more, so we're safe."

He hoped she was right. They followed the blackened wires into the tunnel.

"You know what they say," he chuckled, "that there's people living down here, or at least what used to be people."

Beanie turned towards him, the light from her flashlight flickered across the walls. "That's not true!" she said.

He laughed gently and shook his head. "No, that's not true at all. It's just us down here."

Beanie gave him a long look. They continued in silence.

At the first intersection they decided to remain on the side they were already on, to avoid getting lost. He wondered what would happen if a train did come. Would there be enough space to squeeze up against the dust? Or would they be crushed in the darkness? If that happened, they were already buried. They were currently alive, but buried. That thought made him laugh. His voice filled the black air. Beanie screamed.

"Don't scare me like that!" she said.

"Sorry," he said.

"What's so funny anyway?"

"Nothing." He couldn't tell Beanie his strange thoughts.

He continued walking. The gravel crunched and clattered under his boots.

"Come on, tell me," she said.

"No, I can't tell you. It was just a weird idea."

"Oh, come on."

He hesitated.

"Ok," he said. "I thought if we died here we would be buried at the same time, so it would be a cheap funeral. But then I realized we're already buried, you know, buried alive." He grinned at her. The thought still made him laugh. But he couldn't let it out and scare her more than he already had.

Beanie frowned. "You're crazy, you know that?"

"I know," he said.

They came to another junction. He pierced the darkness of the opposite tunnel with his beam.

"What do you think is down there?"

"Just more rails," Beanie said. "Let's stay on this side. We can't afford to get lost down here."
He thought they could, but maybe they couldn't. They walked until they both had to relieve themselves. Embarrassed, they turned away from each other, and did what they had to do.

"I'm tired," Beanie said. "Let's head back. I think I need to change batteries soon too."

He was disappointed. Nothing had happened. He had only gotten a little scared.

"All right," he said into the warm air. "I can come back another time. Now I know the way."

Beanie stared at him, her flashlight almost blinded him.

"You're not going back here alone. It's too dangerous."

"Shhh...," he said. Even though they hadn't gone as far as he could, they had come as far as she wanted. That worked for him. He shut the torch off and closed his eyes.

In the darkness Beanie said his name. He didn't reply.

His fear of being buried in the stone, of being crushed by gravity, sat like lead in his belly. But there was something behind it; a wall of bone and meat, his own. And an awareness that encircled the tension, watched it and everything else that happened to him. The awareness was more tempting than the tunnels that led into the darkness. He could sense it, behind and surrounding his fear. But neither the fear, nor the darkness, could touch the awareness.

What was it? Was that him? Was that who he was? How could he have missed that? It was too funny. Suddenly, he felt very stupid. He began to laugh. He laughed until his voice rang against the stone. He forgot Beanie until she touched his shoulder gently.

"Please stop laughing," she said. "You're scaring me."

"Me too," he said, "me too."

5: Witness

When he returned to the apartment, he was still disappointed that nothing had happened during the trip. Beanie had been there before and even had a map of the tunnels, a copy of faint blueprints. But it had been fun, regardless.

The day after he felt tired of his job, as he had been for months. Tired of needing the income and tired of not knowing what he would do if he quit. He spent the afternoon thinking about it, turning it over in his mind, hoping to figure out what to do, how to get rid of the tiredness.

In the evening, he was sick of trying to think his way out of the problem, and tried to relax. He was watching some mindless TV when it hit him. Did he lack anything in that moment? Was he lost without the job and the money and the things he thought he ought to have?

As in the tunnel, there was something behind his wants and needs. Something large and still that just watched the desires. He connected with that part of him. He had more questions for it. Who was he without his wishes? What was he without his needs? He watched and waited.

6: Endymion Unbound

That night he dreamed he could fly. He flew up inside a tall tower of brass. From the circular balcony at top, the horizon curved wide. Below him slept a blue and green planet. The oceans and lakes glittered in the sun.

He ran towards the edge of the tower. The air rushed through his wings. He knew he could fly, he had done it many times before. He stepped over the balustrade, and soared high. The horizon tilted as he banked, but his will held. He flew!

The wind rushed in his ears and mingled with the sound of his heart and blood. He shouted with joy and rose in the warm sunlight. He flew out to the blue horizon and the black ocean. He flew until it was night.

The ocean breathed below him. Above him, bright stars pierced the sky. The water was primeval and barren, but he could bring it life. He hovered above the black surface while the wind hissed through his hair. He wanted to put a drop of blood into the ocean to seed it, but realized that wouldn't be enough. However, he had five liters of red inner ocean. That ought to be enough.

The sea wanted it too, and rose up into a dark wall. The black water towered above him, then crashed down and pulled him in. He tumbled and turned and flapped and gasped. The ocean churned him around and around. White bubbles of air rolled around him. Gravity took him down. He plunged into the black and crushing pressure.

But the weight was not stronger than his will, so he remained alive. His long fall ceased at the bottom of the sea. A sandy floor stretched out before him. In the darkness he could sense the presence of long blind worms and round fish with enormous, cauldron-like mouths. Further away, he felt the immense gravity of a deep chasm, an abyss.

He looked up. Through kilometers of dark and heavy water, he saw the stars. They glittered like the corpse lights in the marsh. He let go of the thought of the ocean, pushed away from the cold sand and sped towards the surface.

He woke up and drew his breath once. Then he fell asleep again, but emptied of dreams this time.

7: His Secret Places In The City

1.

The quay reached out into the ocean from the end of the beach that curved along the wide bay. The structure was made of concrete tetrapods piled into the foamy gray water. The long mound of four-limbed shapes was topped with a flat concrete cover. But neither the quay, nor the docks planned east of it, had been finished. The city ran out of money and political will to complete the project. The quay and docks were the remnants of an abandoned dream of urban renewal.

At the end of the unfinished structure the sounds from the city dimmed to a hum. In the white fog the buildings in the city were pale shadows. Below him, the ocean rose and fell, hiding and revealing the lower sections of the concrete. Lumps of yellow foam, a torn plastic bag and pieces of green nylon rope floated on the gray surface. The litter rose and sank with the ocean's breath. Up and down, up and down. A distant horizon separated the gray ocean from the gray sky.

At that secret place, it was easy to relax his hands and open them slowly. His breath and pulse fell.

2.

He remembered a news story about peace-keeping soldiers caught up in a riot in one of the warm cities on the southern continent. When stones and burning bottles fell on the soldiers, they began to fire on the crowd of civilians.

He imagined that the sight of the hot orange sun sinking beneath the hazy mountains at the close of the day, and the smell of the warm dust and human stink of the city, would make a white light rise up inside his mind and blot him out.

He would have been swallowed up by peace, fallen to the ground, while his fellow soldiers shot and screamed. But things like that didn't happen, and the southern continent was far away. It was a stupid story he had to stop telling himself.

3.

The last place was a grove of pines across the lake from the boat club. The club, a white wooden building, rested on top of the gentle slope that surrounded the artificial lake and beach east of the city. In the summer, the club leased small boats and canoes for use on the lake. The building also housed one of the city's best restaurants, busy throughout the year.

His favorite meal there was an appetizer of tatsoi, baby spinach, field salad and rocket salad, with a well balanced vinegar and oil dressing, a main course of tender reindeer filets, the meat sautéed long enough for the outer muscle to have turned brown, but not long enough for it to have gone dry, and a dessert of fresh pineapple flesh soaked in a delicate sugar solution. Rounded off with forest berry sorbet, sweet biscotti, handmade chocolate treats and hot, black coffee.

But in the fall the boats were gone, rain fell as oily drops on the veranda and the wind pulled at the bunched up parasols that stood guard on the slick wood. Across the lake, the pines shook in the floodlights from the boat club.

He wasn't sure how he got there, but his car was idling behind him, so he must have been driving. The icy wind carried needles of sleet that burned his face and hands. He watched the trees undulate in the gale. He was entranced by the way they moved and their willingness to be shifted by the wind, silently and without fear. The trees grew forth from his mind.

8: The Coast Of Bones

Purple, pink and white flowers, their petals nearly translucent, covered the ground, nodded in the warm breeze. The previously dry riverbed he had followed, now carried a wide, shallow stream with a gentle current wafting down the middle. From the banks of the reborn river to the foothills in the distance, the desert was blooming. The sun was hot, but the rain left in his clothes and hair made it bearable.

On the other bank stood a small copse of skeletal trees, budding after the torrent. He splashed across the stream, knelt on the sand and drank from the cool, clear water. He reeled into the spindly shadows of the trees and fell asleep on the new grass.

He expected the bloom to fade, but it didn't recede. He felt no hunger, and when his sunburn healed, there was no discomfort. He stayed in the shade of the trees, breathed and slept. Days turned into nights in a smooth flow of forgetting.

A beach. White sand and white sky. The foam-topped surf rolled ashore unhindered, born by storms far out in the ocean. A seagull hung in the air, pinions white against the sun. The sand was littered with desiccated palm fronds, seaweed and black pebbles; offerings from the sea.

He walked under the jealous sun, but pain was far away. He was reminded of boyhood trips to the coast, of running fast across the sand like he was flying. But this wasn't a trip to the beach. If he didn't find water or reach a village soon, he'd die in the heat. He accepted the thought without regret. He put one foot before the other and kept his pace slow, but constant.

Out there, beyond the hovering seagulls, something dark jutted from the surf like a rotten tooth. It was the stern of a ship, wrecked when it got caught in the currents and hit the rocks that lined the coast like a shark's maw.

The Coast of Bones. If the currents and rocks didn't kill the sailors, and they were lucky enough to pull themselves onto the beach after the crash, the landing would only bring new despair. Inland there was nothing but dunes with tufts of stubbly grass, and then the searing, golden desert going on for an untold distance until the moist vegetation of the rest of the southern continent resumed.

The coast was desolate, a dead man's stretch. There was only the sound of the surf and the wind, the white sand, and the ocean that stretched its agitated waves to the horizon. If he didn't find fresh water soon, he'd die.

He did reach water. The memory of children's laughter, of fishing nets flapping in the breeze, and palm trees shading a group of sheds, remained in his mind. The village had been one of the many he passed in the south and he remembered little from his stay there. But whenever it rained in the city, he missed the Coast of Bones.

9: A Man Of Peace

In his next life he wanted to become a shark; free, fearless, knowing all he needed to know from the start. A white tipped or a black tailed shark. Or a hammerhead with that weird head shape. Most of all he would like to be reborn as a whale shark; a giant with rough, sun-dappled skin, but gentler and more peaceful than his hungry relatives. In his new and liberated form he would roam the seas, from the sunlit upper reaches to the unknown black depths. Even the mightiest predators on the planet, the intelligent apes, would fear the sight of his cutting dorsal fin and vertical tail, iconography of terror, and breathe a sigh of relief as they realized he only ate plankton.

Once, he had tried to communicate with a shark. He went with Katsuhiro to the aquarium in the city. After exhibits with poisonous frogs, yellow sea horses and drab commercial fish, a shallow tank with flatfish and eels, and a moist tropical garden with stick and leaf insects, butterflies and tropical birds, they descended the carpeted ramp of a cold two-story room. The walls were thick glass surrounded by water, a fish tank turned inside out. On the other side of the glass, white and gray sharks rested on the sandy bottom. Only their eyes and gills moved. He wondered how well sharks saw through glass. Maybe they could only distinguish light and shadow?

Some of the sharks' eyes were covered by a white inner eyelid. It made them look old and blind. He hunched down by a large specimen and looked into its eye. The fish moved its eyeball to meet him. For a moment there was a clear awareness of him, but it faded as he was deemed neither threat nor food. He had hoped to see another being looking back at him, but it was like peering into the lens of camera, nothing but an eye.

Disappointed, he moved away. He had thought it would be like the time when he encountered a chimpanzee that sat by the window of its enclosure in the zoological garden. The animal had met his eyes and he had seen a personality glancing back at him. But it might have been the chimp's humanlike eyes and the frown on its forehead that made it look so much like a person.

The lack of recognition in the shark may have been caused by his ignorance of the signaling postures of cartilaginous fish. He might have been wrong. The shark may have tried to communicate with him after all.

Roaming the seas freely without vessel or sails. To see what was far out into the ocean, weeks from land. To know the large sea currents and follow them at will. And to know what was at the bottom of the abyss, see what man had never seen, and be at home there; that was his dream. But when the subject of what people wanted to reborn as in their next life came up at social gatherings, he always said "manta ray, because it looks like they're flying through the water".

10: The Cemetery

For the last seventy years the dead had gone to the new graveyard east of the city. The ground was drier there, which allowed for deeper graves, easier stacking of coffins and faster reuse of the burial plots. The old cemetery by the honeycomb towers had graves and mausolea going back four centuries. It had been up for development several times, but no decision-maker wanted to tempt public outrage by demolishing graves, so the cemetery was left to rot in its own slow pace.

The oaks and beeches, the tall grass and the thick undergrowth made the graveyard seem more like a park than a necropolis.

He hadn't been at the cemetery in a long time, but now he felt drawn to the place. The previous visit had yielded a treasure; a life-sized angel. The angel's kneeling pose, outstretched hands and rain-streaked face had both fascinated and embarrassed him. Now he longed to see the statue again and capture it on film.

He entered the cemetery along the broadest of the two gravel paths that crossed the grounds. He wasn't sure which path he had taken last time, but he had explored all over the cemetery, so it didn't matter which way he took. Rain from the previous night still clung to the grass and trees. The motorway rushed by less than fifty meters away, but the sound was barely audible. It felt like he was on an excursion in the countryside, not two hundred meters from his home.

He followed the path deeper into the cemetery, photographed a squirrel that ran along the branch of an oak, caught the morning light in the curve of a large drop that hung from a blade of grass. The marble and granite headstones had been polished blank by the elements and time. More headstones had toppled than were standing, and the grass grew green and rich around them. He wanted to be buried in a place like that, where people rarely came and the trees grew freely.

Further inside, the footpath merged with its twin. He must be close to the entrance. The path ended in a crescent-shaped clearing. From there he could see the rusted spearhead finials of the gate. The clearing presented a row of small one-story buildings with slanted roofs, columns and friezes - mausolea. Whatever sheen had graced the old marble and granite was gone, the grainy surfaces were spotted with lichen. The glass in the doors and windows was black from pollution and dust. A few worn obelisks stretched to the sky. The grass and ferns reached his knees.

The small structures originated from different eras, most of them had plaques dated two hundred years in the past. The decay gave the buildings an air of gentle melancholy. He tried to capture it with his camera.

His eyes caught the open door before his mind did. He crossed the clearing and stepped over the low iron boundary that encircled the mausoleum. A stock pigeon flew up from the underbrush a few meters away. He was too busy to startle. The door of the tomb was dotted with wormholes. It creaked when he pushed it, but the hinges held. Inside, the air smelled of dust and leaves. With the exception of a few cracked flagstones, the floor was whole.

In the middle of the room sat a large stone sarcophagus with ivy reliefs that curled along the side panels. The lid had heart-shaped leaves on its convex surface, but was otherwise blank, no name or date. He put his palm on the stone and closed his eyes. There was only silence. It was the calm of his own mind. Maybe death wasn't a punishment after all?

He admired the silence for another half hour, then walked home through a soft drizzle.

11: The Empty City

The city and the world revealed itself as empty, with a silence that stretched from eternity to eternity, rendering time and sequence of events meaningless. There was only a never-ending now.

He understood why he liked the unfinished quay and the moving trees so much. That's where he had seen the empty city for the first time.

It was the same world he had lived in since he was born. He had always been inside it, but he hadn't seen it clearly, because his mind was rarely quiet.

It was like stepping out of his thoughts and emotions, to feel pure sunlight on his face and breathe fresh air, with no barrier between the city and himself. He drank from the silence.

12: Rapture

During an afternoon run, he passed a burned out house near the cemetery. The building had been low-income housing, a separate realm of hopelessness and neglect. When the neighborhood was gentrified, a construction company bought the house to reshape it into an apartment building and the tenants were evicted. One night the house burned in arson. The fire also consumed the construction materials on the lot. The arsonist was never apprehended.

The entrance and the lower floors of the house had blown out from the heat and were covered in soot. The fire had melted and twisted the wood and brick, and left cindered beams and gray ashes. Two cable drums, each taller than a man, had also been transformed by the heat. The top halves of the drums were black, the bottom parts still red; the original color of the wire.

The sight of the melted dual-colored wire, the gutted building and the endless sky behind it, sent him into a sudden fit of ecstasy. He threw his head back and fell to the ground. The blue sky watched him and seared him with its beatific space and calm.

He lay on the asphalt, convulsing uncontrollably, but warmly, comfortably. He felt no fear, only a great joy and fascination. He banged his head a few times, but there was no pain. It wasn't strange that he was fully conscious and calm while his body moved in seizures.

An elderly couple spotted him. They rushed to him, asked if he was all right, pulled at his clothes. Unwilling to repress the joy he felt, he didn't reply. The couple thought he had an epileptic fit and called an ambulance. By the time the paramedics lifted him onto a gurney, the rapture had faded and he had regained control over his body. But he was tired and fell asleep on the way to the hospital.

At the emergency room, the doctor asked him to see a specialist to be checked for epilepsy. He promised "yes", but had no plans to see anyone. What he glimpsed and what his body celebrated, was reality itself, the world that was always present. Once seen, that world could not be hidden or forgotten again.

13: Unabated

At night he watched TV, his favorite series on reruns. Suddenly, there was no one in the room, not even him. He wasn't there. Just the furniture and the sounds from the TV and the gray cat asleep in his lap. It looked as if his head had fallen off and there was just a body with arms and legs and a torso that ended in a pair of shoulders. He had no head or face or eyes that separated him from the world. What a strange sensation!

He smiled. He could feel muscles stretch in his face, but the sensation didn't bring his head back. He drew his breath. The air felt fresh and clear, as if he were standing on a peak in the Antarctic.

A ray of light pierced him. He closed his eyes and gaped. He had another shock-like flash before it calmed down.

His head was back, he felt no pain and everything seemed all right. He continued to watch TV while he made plans for the following evening.

14: The Ghost

The underground garage in the honeycomb tower had a rarified light which he liked a lot. The illumination was yellow, but clear, and emitted from fluorescent lamps in the ceiling. The black asphalt on the ground and the gray concrete of the walls, created a backdrop to the light he found both beautiful and harsh.

The smell of exhaust fumes and gasoline added to the skinless atmosphere. The yellow light vanished in the void of the room, between the cars and the ceiling, but reappeared in the surfaces of the vehicles. He stared at it for hours.

When he passed a black almost-SUV, he heard a wail from the trunk. Was there anyone there? More screams, followed by sobs. He turned his head and listened intently. When the scraping started, he realized it was a ghost. He tried to peer through the metal. What did a ghost look like? He had always wondered about that.

He pushed the cold lock, and the lid swung open. The small space was empty, except for a stained mat at the bottom of the darkness. Nothing. He closed the lid. Shrieking and scratching. The ghost wanted to be let out. It was free to go anywhere, but couldn't, because it believed it was still trapped. There was nothing he could do.

He looked at the car. The black metal reflected the yellow light, darkened the shine to a deep golden. It was amazing.

15: The Best Part Of The Movie

One of his favorite movies was scheduled to be shown on TV. Whenever friends and acquaintances mentioned the film, he recommended one scene in particular and eagerly described its symbolism and beauty.

He sat down with a cup of tea, looking forward to watching the movie again. When the scene didn't appear where he remembered it, he became confused, but watched the movie to the end in case it appeared later in the plot.

When the film finished without the scene, he was surprised. He remembered every detail; the characters, the dialogue, the camera panning, the time lapse photography.

Then he laughed. The best part of the movie and he had made it all up after he had watched it for the first time. He wondered how many other of his favorite memories only existed in his imagination.

16: One Of His Friends From University

Last year, one of his friends from university had been hit by a car and spent a long time in hospital. His physical injuries healed, but the emotional damage lingered. To recuperate, the friend went on a holiday to the northern countries, and vanished.

A few days later he received a bubble envelope from his friend, sent on the first day in the foreign, mountainous realm. The envelope contained a small package of dry-cured ham, a delicacy from the north. He opened the package and smelled the thin slices of pork. The fragrance was more mature than in the dry-cured ham he was used to, with an undertone of decomposing flesh. He fried the meat before he ate it.

Now the morning paper told him that his friend had been found. Or rather, the man's rented car and backpack. The car had been parked outside a small bed and breakfast owned by an old couple in a village along a fjord. The young man had last been seen on his way to the mountain behind the village, sporting raingear and looking distant.

It had taken the police months to find the vehicle, because in the spring fifty million cubic meters of mountain fell into one of the fjords in the area, burying the nearest village and several cars on the road. The shockwave created by the tumbling mass of stone and soil overturned two cruise ships and flooded several communities along the narrow body of water. The disaster left a bewildering amount of dead and injured, locals and tourists, and several others missing.

According to the newspaper the old man who owned the bed and breakfast thought the guest had killed himself and was unhappy that he had been unable to lighten the visitor's burden. But the man's wife claimed their guest hadn't committed suicide, despite his backpack having been found in the mountain near an old landslide.

"The mountain took him in," the woman said, referring to a local myth; that sometimes, unhappy people found a deep peace in the mountain and became a part of it. The day press derided the old lady for believing such foolish superstition.

The following afternoon he went to his friend's memorial in the new cemetery and thanked the mountain that had taken him in. It had been the perfect fate for his quiet and perceptive friend.

17: A Force Of Nature

The Earth's crust moved. The magma beneath it streamed and rotated around the searing metal core. He heard the song of the planet, like the ringing of a large bell. It was the sound of the rotation and the currents in the liquid rock.

Then he heard the sun. It sang from the liquid layers that moved in its depths. The vibrations rushed to the surface and exploded into the corona, flaring out in titanic bows that crested high above the burning atmosphere. The song shook the magnetic fields and followed them through space to Earth and beyond.

He thought about nature. All creatures, even man, were part of nature, an embodiment of it. They were forces of nature.

The silence that lived inside him felt like a force of nature ready to rush and run and tear into the world. Was it the primordial force, the original spark from the creation of the cosmos? Could he carry the weight of that spark?

18: Clear-Obscure

He was paddled a small canoe. The coastline was rugged and stony, the white surf broke against the shore. At some places the ocean was still and clear, other stretches were agitated and hard to cross. He knew, because he had been there many times before. He had forgotten the coast when he woke up, but now he remembered. It wasn't a recurring dream, it was a recurring dream place.

The green rim of the canoe rode just above the surface of the water. On earlier trips he swam or paddled, or traveled onboard ferries or cruise liners.

The ocean turned opaque and silent. It was night. In the darkness the sea was obsidian. Despite the gloom, he was surrounded by a faint illumination, like the beam of a flashlight. The brightness followed him as he progressed across the still surface.

Large, orange-red jellyfish appeared in the water. He disliked them. If he tangled the paddle in their veils of tentacles, it would be hard to continue. He tried to avoid the glistening beings, but the jellyfish were large and many. The sea continued to sleep.

The contrast between the beam of light and the dark water made him think of the lighting in classical paintings. The steep illumination scheme was one of his favorite styles of art.

When he woke he marveled at the dream. Even the memory of it was beautiful. He felt blessed to have had a dream in clear-obscure.

19: Evidence

It rained, but the warm precipitation didn't clear the air. It was just as hot and humid as before. The fog grew denser. He slung a thin jacket over his shoulder and left the apartment. He had to see what the trees at the boat club looked like in the fog.

The motorway was empty. The fog reduced driving to a hazard. He could see less than ten meters into the white. Not even the high-rise buildings in the city were visible. It was nearly dark.

He passed the exit to the city and continued east. From the road the boat club windows shone white. He could almost hear the clink of glass and silverware, the hum of quiet conversation, the patrons' steps on the soft carpet, the scent of carefully prepared meals. He ought to take Michael, Katsuhiro, Beanie and Theresa there, get everyone together for a good dinner and some laughs. That would be great.

Past the wooden building and the heavy parasols on the sundeck, he could see the trees. They were waiting for him. He thought about his vanished friend, he would have seen the trees the same way. He had been very perceptive, particularly about nature.

There was no traffic, so he parked on the shoulder and got out. The pines looked as they had in winter, but now the air was hot and humid, instead of stinging cold. He had hoped for a sunny summer, but there had been only fog.

The trees swayed in the wind. Their long needle-covered branches nodded in the moving air. He fell into silence. The shadows spilled over the dark canopies. The floodlights from the boat club lit the pines in gold.

Wind? What wind? The world was covered in fog and the air was still and heavy. He looked at the trees again. They were moving in a wind he could neither feel nor hear. How was that possible? He looked around, but there was only him and the car and the trees.

He phoned Michael.

"Let's take Katsuhiro, Theresa and Beanie to the boat club for dinner," he said. They agreed on a date two weeks into the future.

"I'll make the reservation," he told Michael. He was, after all, standing less than a hundred meters from the restaurant.

He glanced at the moving pines one more time, then returned to the car and continued to the boat club. The night was quiet and dark.

20: The Warming Sky

The building went transparent on him again. From his place inside sleep he saw the stacks of bodies in the floors below.

The sight was still disgusting. He wanted to buy a house in the wilderness, away from anyone else, so he could sleep alone instead of in a rack.

But that night he saw the sky through the floor above him. The ceiling evaporated and gave way to darkness and starlight. The sky looked soft and warm. Billions of stars glistened down at him.

He gazed into space. Each shining point was a star, a star cluster, a galaxy, a group of galaxies; above, around and below him, millions of light years away.

Why hadn't he seen the sky when he first discovered the bodies? If he could see the stacks of sleeping people, he should have seen the stars too. But no matter. He saw them now.

21: Nuclear Blast

He ate after a long, static climb on the horizontal training wall on the top floor. A white light flooded him. The apartment bleached and vanished in the growing brightness.

It looked like he was inside a soundless, painless nuclear detonation. He felt whole and complete. He sat, amazed at the light. It only lasted for a few seconds, then the living room returned.

During the next days he had similar episodes of brightness. The whiteouts didn't last long, just a second or two. He had no warning before they happened and no time to be surprised.

They were his own personal nuclear blasts only he could see.

22: The Cosmic Man I

After the nuclear explosions, it felt like a black hole had opened up inside him and swallowed the cosmos, the entire universe. He felt his surroundings as parts of himself. He didn't dare stretch out to see how far it reached. He already clutched the stars through the ceiling.

Nearby objects were the loudest. He sensed his weight in the sofa, the cold air against the living room window, the electricity that coursed in the lamp next to him. It started raining. The drops spattered the glass and trickled down the surface, smelling of ozone and exhaust.

The drops were cold. He moved his attention elsewhere and no longer felt the rain. Instead, he focused on the heat in his tea cup and the hot air that rose from the TV, and warmed himself. The apartment breathed softly.

He was frightened and overjoyed at the same time. He could sense the world! The empty city had greeted him as itself, embraced him. But it was overwhelming to feel everything. He needed to adjust to it. He watched and waited.

23: The Cosmic Man II

He had to pull his attention away from the world and the objects around him. To distract himself, he thought about the story of the man who stranded on an uncharted ocean planet. The planet was sentient and benign and wanted the shipwrecked to stay. The story ended with the protagonist diving deep into the ocean and merging with the world.

But he thought there should have been more, and imagined another ending:

The castaway witnessed everything on the planet, its cold and fathomless oceans and the strange and ancient creatures that lived there, and almost forgot he had been human. But after a hundred years, the planet became curious about the other worlds in the universe, and if any of them had gained sentience like itself. The shipwrecked returned to his original form, the planet's consciousness still inside his mind.

The planet wrapped his body in a solid, fluid-filled shell and hurled him into space. Inside the cocoon, the castaway held the distress signal transmitter from the ship gently in his hands. After a few weeks in space the pod was found by a cargo vessel.

The crew thought they had found an alien life form and alerted scientists on their home planet. Scans showed that a humanoid figure floated inside the shell. The pod consisted of not previously encountered minerals in different layers, with specific functions. The outer strata were vacuum resistant, the middle folds were shock absorbent, and the inner minerals produced oxygen when submerged in water of the same salinity as the human body.

The scientists sampled fluid from the shell and blood from the organism. Its DNA was 99.75 percent similar to that of human beings. Finally, the scientists cut the pod open with remote controlled scalpels. The ocean water that had protected the shipwrecked flowed out on the antiseptic floor. Cameras hummed and turned to catch every detail of the opening. A man fell out on the tiles, born a second time, coughing warm womb water out of his lungs.

The scientists reeled. After a long decontamination procedure, they woke their guest from his sedated sleep. Although his body had been unconscious, the castaway and the planet's mind had been aware the whole time. When he sat up on the white floor, he knew his surroundings and the people that were watching him. They had only taken the chance of dissecting the pod in a ship in orbit above one of their many worlds.

The shipwrecked opened his eyes and took in the faces that observed him behind transparent, damage-resistant polymer. His eyes were smooth and black, and stars and galaxies burned in them. He was so deeply a part of the cosmos that looking at him was like gazing into space. When the scientists saw that, they screamed.

24: On The Roof At Night

In the evening he had the urge to see and feel the city. He grabbed his raincoat and went up on the roof of the tower.

Rows of ventilation fans spun silently, their noise subsumed into the wind and the rain. He moved across the gravel to the south ledge. There, the view of the city was best. On warm days, Michael and he could sit there for hours, enjoying the pink haze in the sky, trying to catch the sunlight that peered through the fog.

Michael was probably at work or watching his favorite stocks on his laptop tonight. He had been a trader and still followed certain companies. Michael would have loved the view from the roof.

He crouched down and rested his elbows on the ledge. Cold drops congealed on his coat and ran down the fabric. He sat inside it and listened to the water hit the smooth material. The rain calmed him. He could feel the still water in the marsh and the thick grass in the cemetery, but it was distant. The city glowed golden in the downpour. The orange from the high-rise buildings and the white and red on the motorway was so beautiful his body forgot to feel cold.

He remembered the gloom in the tunnels below the train station. The darkness on the roof was different. It was dynamic, noisy and cold, alive and filled with an energy it shared with him. It was much more reassuring than the dead, warm darkness under ground. He wished Beanie were there with him. She would have enjoyed the rain too.

25: Innocence

In the morning he strode through the tower foyer in a good suit, no coat, the laptop in his hand. He passed through the glass doors in a throng and surged with it outside. He'd be in a crowd until he arrived at work.

Inside the school of people, he studied his neighbors. Their faces resembled the visages of children, the children they had been and still were, open and receptive, with clear eyes and round mouths. Their core temperaments and personalities were the same as they had been in childhood, the basic and original reactions unaltered and unalterable.

His neighbors' eyes fluttered back and forth across the world. Did they sense that behind the thoughts and images that flitted by, something remained unchanged, no matter how much motion there was inside the mind or the heart?

At the footpath he walked abreast with two other men. None of them looked at or acknowledged the others. Their steps resounded in the encompassing silence.

26: Musical Day

He hated musicals. He nevertheless had a day full of song and dance.

The alarm clock rang. His gray cat woke and licked his face with a rasping tongue. He turned away from her. The cat purred, butted her forehead against his chin and tried to lie down on his throat. It was time to get up.

On the train to work people slept, read, text messaged, talked, phoned or listened to music. A girl with brown dreadlocks and large earphones reminded him of Beanie. Music pulsed from her silver earphones. When she noticed he was looking at her, she started to bob her head, swing her hips and tap her foot to the music.

In the lunch queue at work, the guy in front of him started singing, something from a musical, he couldn't remember which. At the counter, the cook performed part of an operatic aria before he took his order.

His desk was in the corridor around the atrium in the middle of the building. Because of the sounds and smells from the restaurant and the foyer on the ground floor, the atrium was considered one of the least comfortable places to work. There was also a constant traffic of people on their way to and from the elevators, stairs and hallways. The footsteps made the floor vibrate like a tuning fork. Only trainees and new employees were assigned to the desks along the noisy vertical space.

He, however, preferred the atrium over hot-desking in the stale cubicle halls. Since no one else used "his" desk in the corridor, he had taped notes to the pc monitor, and kept a white miniature orchid, a tray of pens and a cube of note paper on the desk, just like a proper office.

Carla, his boss, said he was presumptuous, but he assured her it was just temporary.

Michael clicked his heels against the floor, spun around while he waved his palms in the air, tie flying, kicked to the right, then to the left, and finished with a finger drum solo on the monitor.

He smirked sardonically at Michael.

"You looked like you needed a little song and dance," Michael said, grinning.

"Join the line," he said.

"So how's it going?" Michael said.

"Great," he said. "Never have so many done so much that meant so little."

"Come on," Michael said. "Be a good little

sociopath. It's work, we get paid. Don't be hysterical."

"If it gets any more meaningless, I might jump," he said.

"Is that why you sit in the atrium?" Michael said.

"I'm pre-empting them," he said.

Michael laughed.

Previous experiments had shown that trying to slither out of work-tasks by delegating them to slower colleagues, or delaying the job by staring at the monitor for hours while tapping the keyboard in mock productivity, didn't make it any more meaningful.

Instead, he performed his duties with the calculated sloppiness of the passive-aggressive, doing just enough, but nothing more. He had been trying to think up something else to do for months, an alternative to his job that had turned more and more odious. For an equally long time he had failed at coming up with something likely.

Later that afternoon someone did try to jump down the atrium, from a floor higher up. Security pulled the man from the glass railing after they distracted him by performing a piece from a famous musical theater.

27: Hysteria

On his birthday before he started school, he received a pencil case from his paternal grandparents. The violet, oblong pouch contained a pencil and a pencil sharpener in the same color. He didn't remember what had happened with the pencil or the sharpener, but he had kept the case for years. He clearly recalled its rough fabric and the school-smell of graphite inside it.

A small bipedal black cat with a large head and eyes was printed on the case. The black cat's world was a solemn sky of violet. The cat stood gazing up, holding a lamp with a flexible neck in one paw.

In the sky flew a tiny black submarine, with its periscope peeking out. Beneath the cat, the word "Hysteria" was written in thin, curving letters; the line of children's stationary the pencil case belonged to.

For a long time he thought that was the cat's name, or the word for the surprise a small black cat feels when it sees a flying submarine. Only years later did he learn that hysteria was considered neither cute nor funny.

28: The House Of Sleep

He worked, exercised and slept. In his dreams he was the essence of all things and the origin of every object.

Steep and snow-covered mountains separated memory from forgetfulness. Lines with devotional flags flashed color in the wind. White temples perched behind rows of rotating copper cylinders on narrow mountain shelves. The temple walls hid burning lotus incense and statues of gold and heavy bells that rang in the booming wind. In the deep cellars monsters roamed unseen.

Below the mountains sat a sunlit plain. There, flowers grew in unceasing bloom and elephants, lions and gnu lived and ate. A broad, indolent river carried melt water from the mountains, split the plain in two. On the far side of the current, gleamed the roof of a small house.

The house was bounded by white gravel raked into simple, geometric patterns. Once per thirtieth heartbeat water streamed up through a crack in a boulder from a pure source. The water filled a bamboo spout until it tipped over with a clap, emptied the liquid into the stream and returned to receive more.

Inside the house, his dreaming self, covered in twelve layers of white silk, sat on the floor and saw with his eyes closed.

He realized why monks sat in meditation. Sitting still and being, instead of doing, allowed the mind to see the world as it was. He had read that there was nothing special with meditation, it was just sitting. And that when he did it, he was real.

The reed mats were warm and smooth and edged with gleaming black silk, embroidered with dragons in silver. Only his slow breath and the breeze lived inside the quiet.

The silence enveloped and embraced him like a lover. He sat. His hair grew down his back and out on the floor.

29: A History Of Violence

He ran. His boots beat hard against the concrete, splayed its skin of water into fans. Rain kissed his face and neck. He was breathing fast. The world moved up and down with each step. He focused and increased his speed. His running pierced the silence.

When he returned from service three years ago, it felt as if his body had died beneath him and become a corpse he dragged around with his mind.

He sensed his body only faintly. He banged his head, stubbed his toes and scraped his knees, because he didn't know where his arms and legs were without looking. His core temperature decreased. His pain threshold grew a lot higher. His sense of smell, taste and touch faded.

During the first months he was frightened. Did he have a nervous breakdown? A delayed reaction to the service? He tried to find a place outside the discomfort and remain there until his body healed, as he had done in training. That only increased the distance between himself and his flesh.

His body never returned to normal. But as the proverb claims, time did heal all wounds, or at least made it more bearable. He became used to his cold and unfeeling corpse. His hearing and eyesight grew sharper. He saw the bedroom with his eyes closed for the first time.

The city offered to protect him. He concealed himself in it, like was used to. The derelict, the abandoned and the forgotten structures welcomed and sheltered him. Lactic acid burn from static or anaerobic exercise allowed him to feel his body when he needed to.

He ran in a long space without ceiling, the top floor of an unfinished building. He followed a wall with square openings at chest height. Outside, palm trees moved in the warm summer gale. Water rushed off the fronds in long, sudden spurts. Behind the palms shone the flat roofs and the square buildings of the warehouse district. The clouds were low and fast.

The wall turned into a ledge. He jumped onto the concrete and followed it through the room. Three floors below, a parallel patch of grass burned green in the muted light.

He ran on the ledge to the stairs and jumped from side to side across the stairwell to descend faster.

The opening at the bottom of the stairs was empty. He rolled out of the entrance onto the wet grass, crossed the street to the next building, ran-climbed a ladder and crossed the district on the roofs.

30: Elven Knowledge

His mother loved fantasy literature. He grew up with stories of enchanted forests, beautiful castles and just kings. Later, he found that he enjoyed the covers of those books more than the stories themselves.

But as a boy he had been fascinated by elves. He admired the elves' fictional love of the land, of beauty and truth, their modesty, self-sufficiency and knowledge of hidden and ancient things.

Now he thought the elves loved nature, because they knew the silence that glowed behind everything. In the still and timeless world, every lake, tree, stone, cloud and blade of grass shone, eternal and new. No wonder elves lived forever!

Last year he had tried an online fantasy game that Katsuhiro worked on and invited him to test. He had enjoyed the long life and the limber body of an elf. Even there the silence existed.

One such place was a large plain of grass. The sky was white and the meadow pale. He travelled across the white field and encountered a great quiet. He knew that around the next group of trees there would be a view of a white plain and a white stream that rested beneath a white sky.

He ran past some blue firs to a hillock and a panoramic view of the area. It was as he had anticipated; calm, white, silent and beautiful. The landscape didn't look real, it was a computer generated simile in three dimensions. Everything inside it had been designed by someone. But he could almost feel the mild breeze and the soft glow of the white sun that was about to set over the grass.

In rapture, he walked on the plain for hours. The sun, artificial and exempt from time, never fell below the horizon, but remained in a poetic spot just above it.

That was, without a doubt, his favorite memory from his time as an elf.

31: Vindication

He was obsessed with a building below the honeycomb towers. The structure looked best in white and rosy dusks in the summer. When the conditions were right, he went to look at it.

The building was a six-story oblong with a slanted metal roof. The ribbed steel walls were stained with rust. Each floor held a row of windows, cloudy glass in thin frames that mirrored the sky. The front door had beveled panels, retrofitted from a home in the suburbs. The structure housed a company that repaired, cleaned and repainted plastic yachts and boats. In the overgrown courtyard, stood the stripped shells of several small craft.

Three of the windows on the fifth floor were open. They slanted outwards at a narrow angle, the glass darker than in the closed panes.

He loved the sight of the building. When he watched it, his heart beat slowly, as if he were asleep. The structure shone inside him. He had taken a lot of pictures of it, but none of them described what he saw.

He imagined standing up there, behind the glass in the lunch room, inside the smell of cold coffee and homemade sandwiches, the kitchen sink matte with grease, breadcrumbs on the formica table in the corner. Orange coveralls smeared with white paint and plastic sealant hung in the nook behind the door. Across the street, a small figure gazed up at the building.

He breathed and watched.

The warm air grabbed the curtains in one of the open windows, pulled the translucent fabric out of the gap and ballooned it out to a round belly. Then it slipped inside to billow through the curtains there, like a wave over smooth stones.

The sight was so beautiful he almost fainted. He watched the curtains move for a long time.

One of the copy writers at work, Per, was a published poet. He lived in the residential area south of the towers, but knew the city well. Maybe he would understand?

At lunch, he sat down next to Per.

"I'm obsessed with this building," he said and held out his phone. "The picture doesn't do it justice, though..."

Per leaned forward and nodded. "Last year, I wrote an article for the newspaper to suggest structures for preservation, the plastic workshop wasn't old enough to go on the list, but I know the place. It's pretty cool."

He was so happy someone else had noticed the object of his obsession, that he couldn't speak.

A few days later, Per addressed him:
> "Hey, that building you like so much…"
> "Mm?"
> "My father-in-law is an architect, and according to him, your building is the most beautiful and interesting in the city," Per grinned.

He laughed, feeling completely vindicated.

32: The Enemy

The nuclear blasts continued. They only lasted for a second, but during that time, he was whole.

At first, the lightning flashes happened a few times a day; right after he woke up, during relaxed swims or climbs, when he ate dinner, or when he was about to fall asleep.

A health check couldn't hurt. He went to the doctor. Heart rate, blood pressure, blood sugar, cholesterol; everything was fine. He persuaded the general practitioner to let him pay a neurologist for an EEG test.

The neurologist, a tall man with ruddy hair and large glasses, placed a net of electrodes on his head.

"You're too healthy," the neurologist joked when the test was done.

He nodded. Never ask a person who sees brain tumors every day whether he thinks you are ill or not. They did have a pleasant discussion about the origins and the location of the personality in the brain. According to science, that was nowhere and everywhere in the organ at the same time. He could have guessed that.

But the blasts became more frequent. He had them ten times a day, twenty and thirty; when he prepared meals at home, talked on the phone at work, or ascended the stairs at the train station in the evening. The white-outs appeared every time he thought about or worried about them. Then he stopped breathing in his sleep.

What should he do? Should he be concerned? Hadn't he invited the flashes in by keeping their possibility, any possibility, open? Hadn't a small part of him waited for the impossible?

33: Heritage

In the hottest and most humid weeks of the summer, the radios and stereos in the city played the same song, over and over. The melody buzzed from digital music players, phones and laptops on the train and at work, in shops, gyms, bars, clubs, cafes and restaurants. It seemed that everyone played or listened to the song. The lyrics were the usual hit music rubbish about lost love and heartache. But the melody was bright and extremely catchy.

When he heard the song for the first time, it stuck in his mind for hours. At first he didn't like the hit, but when he had heard it a few times, he found himself singing along with it. He saw no point in resisting and let the song play in his mind as it wanted to.

He had the song in his head for days. When he woke up in the morning it was there. When he went to bed at night, he was humming it. He even heard it inside his dreams.

Years ago, when Beanie did her undergraduate degree in a small university town up north, he caught the night train to visit her. He bought a bunk, but it was difficult to sleep, because the train braked at curves and tunnels on its way to the highlands. The wheels screeched and clattered, electrical discharges went off from the overhead lines and illuminated the windows in sudden blue.

In half sleep he worried that the train would derail from a stone on the tracks, or tip over in a too sharp bend. When he finally fell away, his heart and breath stopped. It was as if he lost the need to breathe and his body was put on hold at the brink of eternity. He watched and waited. After a while his heart started up again, painlessly and by itself. He was training hard on breath and heart rate control. Perhaps he had overdone it?

Now he let the silly pop song play in his mind and watched and waited, just like he had on the train.

34: A Blue Eye In A Green Sea

He had to live out the rest of his days. How could he do that as close to the silence as possible?

He considered leaving everything behind and go to the mountains, like he had the previous summer.

The image of an inland sea appeared in his mind. The lake glittered blue in an ocean of green. The fluid lens was surrounded by forests of dark spruce. In the summer the air at the lake would be warm and humid. The winters would be dry and icy, with snow thicker than a man's height.

The vision of the inland sea shone in his mind like a jewel. He wanted to search for it and buy a cabin there. He almost bought a train ticket inland to look for the lake, but having no idea where to go and where to start, deterred him quickly.

35: Solace

Michael and Theresa decided he needed a new car.

"I don't even drive to work," he said

"That's no excuse," Theresa claimed.

"Come on, live a little," Michael said.

They took him to a car dealership. Theresa pulled him over to a silver-colored vehicle that gleamed under the store lights.

"That's your car," she said. The vehicle was sleek with smooth curves, almond-shaped headlights and a narrow, triangular grille. It was expensive, but soulless, and said more negative things about its owner than positive.

"I don't like it," he said, although he knew the outcome.

"You'll learn to love it," Theresa said.

"Uff," he groaned.

Theresa laughed at him. Her teeth were so bleached they were tinged with blue.

The car salesman looked too pleased when he signed the contract. He wanted to punch the guy, but it wasn't his fault he bought the damned car. The keys felt cold and heavy in his hand.

He took Michael and Theresa to the boat club as planned. On the way they picked up Katsuhiro and Beanie. They had to wait for Beanie outside aunt Margrethe and uncle Mads' house. Margrethe came out on the stairs and waved at them.

"Come see our new car!" Theresa yelled in their mother's and Margrethe's language. Margrethe smiled and approached the vehicle.

"Congratulations!" she said. "It's a very handsome vehicle"

"Thanks, aunt Margrethe," he said.

"It looks fast. Please drive carefully with it."

"I promise."

Margrethe turned towards the house. "Beatrice!" she yelled. "Your cousins have waited for five minutes already! Where are you?"

"Here! Stop nagging mom!" In the open door, Beanie tugged her pink sneakers on. She pulled at the laces as she jump-limped to the driveway.

"Take your time, Beanie," he said. "We're not in a hurry."

"Did you reserve a table?" Theresa said. "I hear the boat club is busy these days, with the weather we're having."

"Yeah, at seven."

"Nice car," Beanie said and climbed in. "Do you

like it? Theresa and I picked it out for you last week."
She grinned at him in the rear view mirror.

"*Et tu, Brute*," he sighed.

Beanie laughed.

At the boat club he glanced at the pines across the lake,
and was relieved he couldn't see if they were moving or
not. The company of his siblings and cousins was bright
and warm. When the dinner was over he took the tab.

He had a long, slow morning in bed with Michael. Then
Michael wanted to go to the quay.

"Are we getting your fishing gear first?" he said.

"No, let's just go," Michael said.

It looked as if the sky wanted to rain but couldn't
get it to happen. The road along the ocean was empty,
save for a few other cars.

On the beach they passed joggers, strollers and dog
walkers. The ocean rolled heavy, foam-topped waves
ashore. They walked barefoot and let the cold water sear
their skin. Michael pushed his heels into the sand. The
footprints were visible after the first and second wave,
but the third erased them completely.

At the end of the quay they sat down. The ocean rose
and fell in a slow rhythm. A small wind came in from the

sea. He thought he saw the horizon through the gray wall of mist, but that couldn't be right. The fog was thicker than that.

36: Subsistence

That night, inside sleep, he saw a spiraling cosmic cloud. The hazy disc circled itself like a hurricane and grew thicker and denser. From the center of the cloud came the same dizzying tug as from the deep ocean when he was pulled from the sky.

He thought he was going to be dragged under again. Instead he felt a tremor, like distant thunder. The cosmic cloud contracted and a white spark flared up inside it. He had time for a second of concern before a brilliant ray shot out of the disc in both directions. The white light spiraled fast, dust and gas swirling around it.

He got the ray in his chest. It exploded up his spine and made his back arch violently. He cried out. The white fire rushed into his head and dissipated. His thoughts and emotions bled out with the ray. Then he fell into a quiet, dreamless sleep.

37: Reckoning

In the oldest section of the city, a small park hid between the buildings and the motorway ramps. The garden included an old house brought piece by piece from his father's country, and a circular pond. The park had started life as a simile of carefully tended, traditional gardens. But now it was neglected and overgrown and only received the brutal shearing the city visited upon all parks twice a year, once in summer and once in winter.

The garden was a small jungle of maple, gingko, hazel, oak and bamboo trees. The grass in the middle of the plot had been mowed down to dry and yellow tufts. Outside the perimeter of cut lawn, the vegetation stood tall and flowering.

The house was small, the size of a modest apartment. There was a large hole in the once carefully thatched roof. Gray clouds rushed by in the overcast sky. The wind brought the scent of cut grass and decaying plants.

He entered the structure. The floor was littered with glass shards, beer cans, rotting grass and pebbles. A pair of dirty jeans had been discarded in a corner. The room stank of urine and beer. The far wall held a broken window. Through it, he could see a disheveled grove of bamboo move in the wind.

There was nothing there for him. The house felt no closer to the silence than his own living room did. He wasn't sure what he had hoped to find.

He turned towards the entrance. Through the empty opening he saw the brown heads of the cattails by the pond and a short wooden pier that led out into the gray water. Above the trees and bushes shone a pewter sky.

The sight quieted him. The silence existed everywhere. He didn't need to chase it.

He walked to the pier. The old wood creaked and the wind pulled at his hair and tie. He sat there for a long time, dangling his feet over the choppy water under the gray sky.

38: Into The Heartland

During lunch in the first floor cafeteria at work, his boss, Carla, told him she was afraid of lucid dreams.

"What's that?" he said, curious about what scared her.

"Dreams where you know you're dreaming and then changing the dream," Carla said. "Sounds too much like self-hypnosis and playing around with sanity to me. I don't understand why people try to have them."

"Doesn't everyone have that kind of dreams?" he said.

Carla looked at him over her trendy, dark-rimmed glasses. "I don't know," she said. "There's a lot of books and manuals about it."

He wanted to hear if she had seen anything about recurring dream places while she read about lucid dreams, but thought it best not to ask.

Carla's information surprised him. He had been able to remember his dreams well, to know that he was dreaming, and to change his dreams, for as long as he could recall.

As a child he had a recurring nightmare where he was chased by an unknown enemy. When he tried to run away from the shadow, it slowed and caught him. He woke from the bad dreams with fluttering heart, feeling sick from fear and frustration.

But even as a five year old boy, he knew he was the proprietor of his own dreams. The next time he was chased, he was ready. He stopped and turned towards the dream enemy and wished him away. Or he created a large pit that opened up behind him and swallowed the chasing shadow. Or willed the dream to let him run faster, or slip away through a hidden door. He couldn't change everything in the dreams, but he could alter how he reacted to uncomfortable events.

Then he wanted to fly. Once he understood that remembering the wish was necessary to translate it into reality in dreams, he began to fly. First haltingly and without much control. At times he fell from the sky like Icarus, or couldn't find the lightness of mind to ascend more than a few meters. But after a while, he threw himself from towers and mountains, and soared over rooftops and oceans.

He didn't reflect much on his control of dreams. He assumed everyone else did the same, that it was one of those things you just didn't talk about.

39: A Dream In The Forest

In his dreams he followed a path of exposed bone through a snow-dusted forest surrounded by winter mountains. The forest's heart hid a white city that reflected the sun. The light reminded him of the few winters when they had snow in December, and of the rarified, high-altitude illumination he had seen in pictures from the mountain ranges in the east.

He decided to enter the city with impunity. Its pale outer wall was clasped shut with a gate of solid brass. The defenses were high and smooth, with no handholds for intruders. Standing before them, he felt like a little boy who tried to get a glimpse through a high window.

But why not try the direct approach and use the door instead? He took hold of the bottom edge of the gate and pulled hard. A deep boom rang through the structure. The metal moved, just far enough for him to slip inside.

A long boulevard pointed towards the city center. The wide thoroughfare was lined with tall statues that wore stern stone faces and white marble robes. An icy wind blew from the snow-covered mountains.

The boulevards, statues and buildings were smooth and whole, but covered in fine dust. His shoes left faint prints. The city's walls, doors, pilasters, colonnades, domes, benches, fountains and agorae were decorated with graceful, intricate curves and curls. At first, the design looked beautiful and his eyes followed the patterns willingly. But there was no variation, and even beauty repeated was monotonous to watch, like a person dressed in all designer plaid.

He yawned. Had the city been abandoned? He saw neither living nor dead, not even remnants of dead. He searched several apartments and houses, even a few palaces. The rooms were sparsely furnished and decorated in the same single-minded style as the exteriors.

But he saw no corpses, no blood, no weapons, or traces of struggle. Instead, he found tables with bread, meat, vegetables, cheese, fruit, wine and beer. The food looked almost fresh, as if it had been abandoned yesterday.

In the basement of a house he spotted three sturdy paper tubes with long fuses of twine, handmade firework rockets, propped in a corner. When he touched their grainy surface, he heard the sound of thunder and his vision blurred, as if he were under water. He carefully tilted the rockets back into the nook and hurried out of the house.

Tired of the cold city and the smooth marble, he returned to the gate. He squeezed out of the opening and pushed the brass shut. The gate closed with a resonance that trembled through his body.

He turned towards the bone path and the white forest. The sunlight afforded a small warmth and the breeze carried the scent of fresh snow. It was good to be out of the dead city.

Someone tugged at him, like a child. A small green creature squinted up at him and smiled, revealing two rows of pointed teeth.

"Hello..., goblin," he said, needing a second to remember what type of being this was. The wily-looking creature nodded up at him and lengthened its grin. Was it going to bite him?

"An elf! An elf!" the goblin squeaked.

He looked around in alarm. Was the goblin calling his friends? But there was only dust and forest and white wind.

"Hush!" he said. "I'm not an elf, just a visitor. What are you doing here? Invading, maybe?" He smirked at his own joke.

"You not make fun of me! Not make fun!" yelled the goblin. "The orcs took the stronghold a long time ago, but there was no one there. Without elves, the place was no fun, so we left."

He thought of the large, empty construction and laughed in the frozen silence. The winter air was so invigorating, everything seemed funny and without consequence.

The goblin looked at him with large eyes. "You are funny and happy. Do you want to be an elf and live here?"

"An elf?" he said, chuckling.

"Yes! Have many strong sons and build an army and then fight! Fight fight fight!" The thought seemed very appealing for the green creature.

"Fight the orcs?"

"Yes," the goblin said. "Claim the city and become god! King! High priest! Whatever you want to be."

"I know," he said. "But you, my friend, are not an orc."

The goblin sniffled. A green tear ran down its rubbery cheek.

"I could be," the goblin said.

For a moment he considered it, playing a game of honor and loyalty that would last ten thousand years or more.

But he had no inclination to be bored for that long, not even in his dreams.

"You are aware that you are in my dream now?" he asked the creature.

"I am not inside your dream!" the goblin said. "Not at all! It is you who are here! A kingdom independent from all others and rightly ruled by ..."
The goblin's long and intricate explanation faded into sleep. When he woke up he was still laughing.

40: Shadow War

There was another place he had to visit. He had thought about it for some time, but not dared to go there. Now he considered it unavoidable, a *fait accompli*. That knowledge was frightening in its absolute decision. But it was also easy to accept, because it had already taken place. Maybe that was why some words, some places and some people were frightening? They brought to light what was going to happen, what was already underway and what was unavoidable.

He drove out of the city with only the camera and a bottle of still water in his backpack. The site was well known among explorers and photographers. He had even heard stories about it at work, but few seemed to have been there.

The day was sunny and clear. The white fog had lifted and the weather turned colder and less humid. Fall was in the air, even though it was early July.

He parked behind some pines so the car would be less visible from the road. He regretted having gone along with Theresa and Michael's choice of car. Now he had to worry about both the vehicle and the insurance, and make sure he didn't lose any of them.

He shouldered his backpack and faced leviathan. It was five stories tall, with a massive midsection and two identical wings. It had been built as a tuberculosis hospital, but when the white plague no longer haunted the population, the construction had served as a psychiatric facility instead.

Both sides of its past frightened him. The thought of being confined to a hospital, with thousands of others who suffered from the same incurable disease, with no prospect of getting out, scared him. Being incarcerated and not in control of one's mental faculties, frightened him even more. But now he had to go to that place voluntarily, to test himself against it.

The gate was flanked by a low stone fence that he easily crossed. Grass, clover and golden Birdsfoot Trefoil flowers peeked through the white gravel in the driveway. In front of the main stairs sat a circular concrete fountain, its pump rusted black. The basin had cracked and grass widened the scar. When he saw that the smiled. He took a few shots of the front and the fountain.

The building loomed above him. The windows he could see were barred and broken. A broad flight of stairs led up to two beautiful, massive doors in curving *art noveau*-style. The doors were pinched together with a chain and padlock, but stood ajar, dead leaves and sand amassed between them. He ducked beneath the chain and entered.

The foyer was brightly lit by three lancet windows in the grand staircase at the back of the room. Dust danced in the sunlight. The floor had checkered tiles and an *art noveau* counter with curling, rounded corners. He photographed the desk, the arched windows and the golden shafts of light. How many people had died in the building during the half century it had been used? Five thousand? Ten thousand?

He continued up the stairs. On the third floor landing were two doors with panes of wire glass and thick black letters: "Personnel only. No admittance." The sky blue paint was blistered and chapped, and shed in flakes on the grimy floor. The left pane had a spider web break.

The first and second floor had housed offices and common rooms, and the patients that were the least ill and still able to take strolls outside. The third, fourth and fifth floors were the real hospital. Like a boy dreading the cold sea on a summer's day, he decided to immerse himself slowly. He started with the third floor.

The blistered doors were unlocked. Glass from the broken pane crunched underfoot. He peered into the corridor. Sunlight streamed in from the open doors along the hallway and obscured the end of it. Sand, leaves and paint flakes littered the floor. The air smelled of dust and old age.

He continued into the corridor while he documented the wonder of decay around him. The sunlight warmed his face. Each door was a wooden slab with a barred opening high up and a small hatch near the bottom, just like in a prison. He smiled. The city, with its bright, hurrying life, was just a few kilometers away, and here this silent behemoth sat, just waiting for people to come and lose themselves in it.

He entered the rooms. He didn't dare think of them as cells. They were tall and narrow and had a metal bed with a rotting mattress, a wooden desk by the window and a small porcelain sink behind the door. Some rooms had lidded metal buckets in place beneath the sink. The institution-green walls were blistered and cracked. Other rooms had old lamps, milky white oblongs with gilt edging that resembled lace, still sitting in the high ceiling. They made the rooms look beautiful and antique. He photographed them obediently. It looked as if the building was showing itself from its best side.

Down the hall he found a shower room with cracked tiles, the summer breeze drafting in through broken and barred windows. The stalls hid split pipes, crooked faucets and old shower heads. Rust and mildew crept along the walls. He doubted there was any water left in the veins of the old house.

Still further in, he found spacious rooms with file cabinets, lamps and desks. One room had a beautiful, high-backed wheelchair that squeaked loudly when he lowered himself into it for some self-portraits. The sun glinted in an old metal lamp lying on an overturned desk.

From the shattered window he could see a large meadow bounded by the stone fence and pine forest. The roof of his car gleamed in the afternoon sun. Good. It was still there.

He left the large rooms and returned to the third floor landing. Instead of the tall windows on the first floor, the sun squinted through tiny openings of frosted glass in the stairwell. He passed the fourth floor landing and continued up to fifth floor. There, a metal ladder with a rusty railing led to a trapdoor in the ceiling. An arrow-shaped mound of glass shards and pebbles aimed at the ladder, a point of interest indicated by earlier explorers. It had to wait. He had to see the fifth floor first.

He got what he had come for. The patient rooms on the top floor resembled those below. But the larger rooms had gurneys stained with rust, and tables with broad leather straps and metal headbands. Colored wires connected the headbands to electrodes, consoles and monitors gray with dust. One table had a tray of old surgical tools, including two long needles with a crescent-shaped head. He photographed everything. He regretted that he hadn't invited Beanie along, she would kill him when she saw the pictures.

When he had witnessed the signs of old psychiatric methods, and the rooms and the cells for himself, his fear faded. Much suffering had taken place there, but like the fountain, nature had reclaimed the building. The past was gone, there was only the present. Now people just came there for excitement and curiosity, like he had.

Something blocked the light from the doorway and disappeared. He turned and ran to the door. The sunlight from the rooms across the hall blinded him. He thought he heard running steps.

"Wait!" he shouted, dropped his camera into the backpack and started running. He saw traces of flight, a door vibrating on the frame like it had just been glanced, leaves and dust kicked up in the air, scuffmarks in the paint flakes on the floor. The door to the landing rattled. He knew where the other was going. He jumped from the doorway, grabbed hold of the railing and ran up the shaking ladder. He reached the ceiling just in time to catch the thin trapdoor as it fell. He pushed against the metal, flung it aside and vaulted up into the sunlight.

The roof had a coarse sandpaper-like surface for traction. A few skylights were visible here and there, but otherwise the roof was empty. He continued towards the edge. There was no railing or balustrade, only a ledge and a fall and the yellow meadow below.

There was someone behind him! He twisted around, but received a good push before he was safe. He fell sideways over the edge. For a moment he saw only sky and grass and was certain he'd fall. But his body reacted faster than his mind. His flailing hands found a hold and grabbed hard, straining his arms and shoulders painfully. He slammed into a wall and heard glass shatter. The tip of his boot had found an unbroken pane in a window below.

He hung from the bars of a window on fifth floor. He inhaled to get the fear out and the climbing going, tensed his muscles against his own weight. It was a measure that was deeply familiar to him from hours on the gym wall. The sunlight dimmed as a head blotted it out.

"Come and get me!" he shouted, blood up. Not only did the attacker push him off the roof, but checked to make sure he was gone! He heaved himself onto the window ledge and took hold of the roof to climb back on it. Lightning pain shot up from his hand as his attacker stomped on it. He yelled and automatically let go with that hand. It felt like some of the fingers were broken. But he knew how many fingers he needed to hang on with and how many he needed to advance.

He grabbed his opponent's pant leg with his good hand and held on through the pain. The assailant stumbled backwards and wrenched free from his grip, but he had already gotten the momentum he wanted. He kicked hard from the window and vaulted up on the rough surface.

Nothing. Nothing but sky and sun and air and a faint rustle of wind in the trees below. He scrambled to the trapdoor. It was shut tight. He swore and stomped the iron. He ran along the edge of the roof and scanned the wall for a service ladder. There, a rusty old thing. He kicked it. The metal shook loudly, but seemed to hold. He had to take the chance.

He flung himself on the ladder, kept the crook of his wounded limb around the oxidized metal, and slid down. It didn't make his hand any happier, but he got down feet first.

He vaulted over the stone fence and ran to the car. The vehicle looked like it had when he left. There was no one in sight. Not a flutter of leaves or a shadow passing. He bent forward and tried to open his hand. Damn. He might need surgery.

The car alarm went off. The sound sent a shock through his body. A flock of sparrows rose from the trees behind him. For a moment he was scared, but the fear quickly transformed into humor. There was no one there but him. The car sensors had reacted to his motion and presence. He leaned against the car and laughed the tension out. Maybe he had anticipated everything and made it happen? Perhaps he had created the situation himself?

He shut the alarm down and drove slowly back to the city. Even on the roof the silence had enveloped him, embraced his fall and climbing. When he thought of that moment, of hanging over the ledge with one hand, looking up into the blue sky, a brilliant light flooded his mind.

41: Reset

When he told Beanie about his visit to the sanatorium, she just smiled.

"It's an awesome place," she said. "Did you like it?"

"I did." He looked at her. "Are you angry that I didn't ask you to come along?"

Beanie shook her head. "I went there last year with some friends."

"Without me?"

Beanie laughed. "You were working so hard and we kind of went on a whim. I'm sorry."

He smiled at her.

"We're planning a trip to the old airfield next weekend," Beanie said. "Rumors say there's a large bunker with tunnels. Come with us."

"I can't," he said. "I have a date with your brother next weekend. Besides, I'm no good exploring right now." He held up his right hand, which he had tried to bandage with his left.

Beanie grinned. "Poor baby. What did the doctor say?"

"I set it myself," he said.

Beanie frowned. "If it heals badly, you have to break it up again."

"I know." His hand was throbbing and he didn't have any painkillers.

Beanie rose. "I need to run," she said. "Meeting Eric in half an hour. Thanks for the coffee and the fun story. You have to post the pictures soon."

"I will," he said. "When I can use a mouse again."

"Feel better soon." Beanie kissed him on the cheek, pulled on her jacket and boots.

"Please don't go to the airfield," he said when she exited the door. "There's a lot of old drums there, leaking chemicals..."

"Yuck," Beanie said. "I didn't know that. Maybe I'll skip it. Eric wanted to see a movie too."

"Good girl," he said.

"Take care," Beanie said and closed the door.

He did need surgery for his hand. In the evening, it swelled to twice its normal size. The pain was a constant throbbing in his mind and he could barely move the arm. Swearing, he put his shoes and jacket on and drove to the emergency room.

He had to stay over night at the hospital for observation, in a room with three empty beds and an old telephone. In the morning they x-rayed his hand and sent him to an orthopedic surgeon.

The surgeon paralyzed his arm by anesthetizing a nerve center between his shoulder and spine. He asked if he could watch the procedure. The nurse looked at the physician.

"Why not?" the surgeon said. "It might make you see a doctor first next time, and if you faint, you're already lying down."

His three middle fingers were opened under a battery of regional anesthetics and painkillers. The moist bone and cartilage gleamed in the bright light. The surgeon pulled out small fragments from the breaks, then realigned them like shattered pottery and drilled a fine wire through it to hold everything in place. Finally, the pieces were fastened with narrow plates and tiny screws on the surface of the bone.

At two fractures, the surgeon teased the fragments out from behind the break with an angled wire and filled the area with growth factors, before he realigned the bone and plate it together.

When the procedure was over, his hand looked partly mechanical, with a spread of metal plates and screws holding his fingers and joints together. But despite the alterations to his hand, he felt the same as before. He was clearly not his body.

"Now you only need three weeks in a splint and a lot of physical therapy," the surgeon said as he stitched the last finger.

"Three weeks?" he groaned.

The surgeon looked at him. "Compression fractures can't be reset like that, even if you think so."

"Will I be able to play again?"

The surgeon laughed. "If you give your hand the rest it needs and do the physical therapy exercises, your hand will be fine. No thanks to yourself. Next time, see a doctor first."

"Yes, sir."

"How did it happen?" the physician said.

"Loose rocks on a climbing trip," he said. "Was lucky they didn't hit my head."

The surgeon's eyes narrowed in a smile.

The doctor put his hand in a metal splint to keep the fingers bent at the right angle, then wrapped it in a thick support bandage that reached up to his elbow. Katsuhiro drove him home, then returned to work.

He took the painkillers he had been prescribed and went to bed feeling puffy and strange. The splint and the bandage added to the claustrophobic sensation of disability. He fell asleep in his bathrobe. When he woke, it was four in the morning and he was lying on the cold gravel of the tower roof. He was never going to take painkillers again.

42: Creativity

"Do you think we can come to create what we expect?" he asked Katsuhiro the following night. His brother had come to check on him. They were watching TV together.

"Like attracting things?" Katsuhiro moved his sharp focus of attention to him.

"I mean in general, not wishing for specific items or events."

Katsuhiro thought. "Yes, I think so," he said. "The way we view the world influences how we relate to it and even what happens to us. I really think so."

He nodded. "Me too."

Katsuhiro smiled.

He wanted to tell Katsuhiro what had happened at the abandoned hospital, but letting his brother know that he had almost fallen off the roof because of someone who might or might not have been there, would only upset him.

Katsuhiro disliked his hobbies enough as it was. When he had told him about the trip under ground with Beanie, Katsuhiro had admonished him not to go there again. At such times his younger brother looked very much like their father.

43: Cats And Places

He hadn't always seen the empty city, but he suspected that a part of him had been aware of the silence since childhood and tried to find it.

Was that why buildings and landscapes had always seemed as important as people?

His mother said that cats were attached to places, not people. His memories were tied to places and their architecture and space. Did cats feel the same?

44: Testify

When he was ten years old, he did something terrible. But common sense said that he couldn't have done what he thought he had. Thus, he couldn't tell anyone, and it became his secret.

His mother took him with her on a visit to a friend and her daughter. The daughter had epilepsy and was taking medicines for it. The medicines were strong, but the girl hadn't had a fit for years. That made him curious about epilepsy. He'd heard about it, but never seen it.

When the adults sat enjoying their coffee and cake in the sofa at the friend's house, he drank his red lemonade with a green plastic straw and gently pushed at the girl's mind. He thought she was weaker than him and receptive. He pulled at something in her, like a small trapdoor, and waited.

The girl fell off her chair, shaking and shivering. Her mother sprang up and put her in a stable position. He watched them silently from his seat, while he slurped lemonade through the straw. His mother wanted to call for an ambulance, but her friend stopped her. The girl had been symptom free for years, but she hadn't taken her medicines for a while.

"It's probably time we see a doctor and get back on them," his mother's friend said.

They left after that. He put on his down jacket and the hat and gloves his mother had knitted for him, and walked next to her in the snug autumn darkness.

He decided to limit experiments to himself. The next summer, he taught himself to dive and swim under water. He went with his brother to a nearby pool every day and stayed there for hours. When he returned to school in the fall, he frightened his gym teacher by swimming for so long under water that she forbade him to do it again. She yelled at him from the edge of the pool, but under water her voice was slow and thick and without consequence. He pretended he couldn't hear her and continued to swim.

45: An Empty Cipher

He was an empty cipher, a colorless color. His family and friends talked to a mind with no fixed content, just scattered memories and a collection of habits and tendencies.

It was a heap with an empty core. Past the horizon of acknowledgeable events he was a black hole of not-knowingness.

He went for a walk. The towers and footpath and park waited quietly inside the silence. They had their faces turned towards the sun. His thoughts danced on the wind like a kite on a long string.

46: The Rain On Titan

He wanted to harden his skin and the surfaces of his eyes, throat and lungs, rip free from Earth's gravity, and hurl himself into space.

Escape velocity. He liked that term. Escape, fly into space and be gone. Then witness the sun set on Mars, volcanoes erupt on Venus, ice crack on Europa, and the dawn rise on Pluto, where the star at the center of the solar system would be an almost forgotten memory.

According to science, Titan, Saturn's largest moon, had a solid surface with mountains and hills and plains, just like Earth. Its atmosphere contained nitrogen, methane and helium. The moon was so cold the methane stayed liquid. The seas and lakes and rivers on Titan ran with methane instead of water.

The methane evaporated and condensed into clouds. Because of the low gravity, the rain collected in large drops that fell to the ground as slowly and softly as snow on Earth. He would have given everything to see the rain on Titan.

He decided to dream about traveling the solar system. The night was filled with dreams, but when he woke up he could only remember trying to lift a corpse on a door over a chain link fence.

47: The End Of The World x 2

The apartment was quiet and his hand throbbed. He needed extra sleep to heal, so he indulged in it to new heights. But his dreams were not good. He dreamed about the end of the world.

In the first dream, he was part of a theater troupe that rehearsed a darkly comic play about the end of days. They met in a basement in the city. The other actors were strangers. Despite the somber theme, the atmosphere at the rehearsal was friendly and upbeat.

His role was the angel that heralded in the end of the world with a golden trumpet. He followed the other characters; the ordinary young couple caught in the doomsday mess, the judge who tried to make a difference, evil himself and his demonic friends, and the choir of supporting angels, and commented on the events.

The plot described the follies of creator, man, good, evil and religions. He played his part with a smile, cavorted around with white feather wings and a golden *papier-mâché* trumpet, and made sly lines as the gates to the end were opened, one by one. His sister had been right when she said angels would be the next big thing after vampires.

But then the dream turned serious and he realized he wasn't rehearsing doomsday for a play, but for the world. He was surprised, but kept making happy trumpet sounds into his horn. He had to play his part well.

He woke up with the fanfare going in his head, as well as the path he had planned across stage past the unlucky couple and a group of minor demons.

When he went to bed that night, he had forgotten about the doomsday play and was only looking forward to sleeping. But then it was time for the end of the world again.

The city was deserted. He roamed the streets and wondered where everyone had gone.
The stars were faint and distant, and the moon a sickly yellow. Only a few squatters were around, in doorways and on street corners, they looked just as lost as him.

He didn't know where to go or what to do. The maker's voice vibrated to him on the wind, told him not to be afraid, but to relax and let things unfold as they had to. It was the end of the world and there was nothing he could do.

When he heard that, he became frustrated. Why did he have to live through the end times? What wrongs had he done to experience it? He tried to keep his courage up by repeating the prayer about the valley of death, but it didn't help.

He took refuge under one of the city's rail bridges, deeply disappointed that he had ended up there, despite his efforts at being successful in life. He was frightened, even though he suspected that he was asleep.

At the end of the dream, he tried to evacuate people in an old tourist ferry, because part of the judgment was a greatly elevated sea level. When he woke up, he felt sad and drained and it took hours for the dream to fade.

48: Burn White

The white fog closed over the city again. It was humid and hot. He took a nap during the day, the cats curling up next to him in bed. He slept for too long. When he woke up, he was drowsy and dull, and his hand ached.

He staggered to the kitchen and filled a glass of water in the sink. There was only the glass, the sink, the running water and the muted sunlight, no him.

Every time he fell asleep, his feeling of self vanished. But maybe that was a wrong description, a wrong view? Maybe his self didn't vanish, but had never really been there in the first place, like a dream? How could he find out?

49: Coming Up Roses

An old dream, recurring since his teens. The sky was gray and the ground was gray. In the slate-colored foredawn, dark clouds rushed by. He stood on a cliff above a surging, foaming ocean.

Behind him sat a long two-story building. The entrance was tucked behind four weather-worn columns supporting a veranda. The ground floor was a row of casement doors with broken panes. Rose bushes raked the gray walls with their thorns. He knew what he was going to do, what he always did in that dream.

He slowly approached the roses. They shone arterial red in the windy gloom. His gloves were thinner than the skin of his eyelids. He peeled the fabric off one hand and picked a rose. It pierced his skin deeply and a dark drop blossomed out. He lifted his hand and licked the blood, while the wind screamed in his ears.

The blood, the sting and the feeling of the rose petals between his fingers overcame him. He fell to the ground in a paralyzing swoon and lay in the cold wind for a long time.

The bedroom was dark. His heart was pounding, his neck and chest wet. Thunder rolled across the sky. The cats gave him sullen glances and jumped down from the bed. He wiped his skin. He could smell himself, a deep animal musk. His mouth tasted of blood, although his thumb was whole and smooth. He felt aroused and queasy at the same time.

The gray curtains rose and fell in the draft from the open window. The predawn darkness was warm and humid, the light from the city shone faintly in the fog. He thought of the pines by the boat club, but shrank from the idea. He was too tired to go and watch them now. He turned the pillows to the dry side and tried to return to sleep.

Part 2 – Giving In

50: A Single Day Of Happiness

As a boy he believed that if he had one day of complete happiness, he would know how to be happy for the rest of his life. For a long time he carried the belief at the back of his mind, quietly hoping it would take place.

As he grew older, the idea faded and he only recalled it when he was in his mid-twenties. At that point the notion of having a day of complete happiness seemed ridiculous. No day would be completely happy, no matter how many good things happened that day. He felt silly to have believed something like that.

He had long since relinquished the idea of having a day of complete happiness, when it happened.

He got up earlier than usual, showered with the splinted hand in a plastic bag, had a quick breakfast of cereal and rice milk, and caught a taxi to the airport. He flew for fifty minutes through thick white fog and landed in a city further up the coast. There, he met with colleagues in that city's branch of the company.

Carla had called earlier in the week to remind him about the appointment, and to ensure that he went.

"I'm on sick leave, remember?" he said. "I can't

type or write." It felt both titillating and frustrating to point out his newly acquired helplessness.

"You don't have to," Carla said. "Just shake hands with your left, give out your card and smile. You still remember how to do that, don't you?"

"Barely," he said, smirking.

At the meet and greet, his colleagues commended him for work he had done earlier in the summer. He was pleased, but felt he could only take part of the credit. Before he had started the task, he knew what the finished result would contain and what it would look like. It had already been created, he just had to get it into the world. It was another *fait accompli*.

The dinner was pleasant, with friendly chatting and good food. He had prepared a brief climbing story to explain the splint and the sling, and embellished it with gory details from the surgery. That prevented more questions about the accident.

Then it was time to leave and board the plane back. Another near hour of fog, the captain gunned the engines and landed fifteen minutes ahead of time. The pilots obviously wanted to go home early too.

In the apartment, it hit him that he had been happy the whole day. He had been sleepy in the morning and tired when he returned, but his mood had been light since he woke up. He had simply been happy. When he realized that, a bright brilliance sprang up inside him and filled him with a golden light. He reeled and supported himself on the kitchen counter. Would his life end, now that he had had his day of complete happiness?

The TV blared on and it was moist and humid. When would the weather change? In the fall? The winter? Never? Would he live out his remaining years under eternal fog? Somehow, that felt fitting.

His thoughts came and went, and he was still breathing.

"That's it," he concluded. The moment had appeared and vanished. His childhood wish had come true. It felt as if he had been touched by grace.

After that, it was easier to open up to happiness, to joy without specific reasons. It was good to just be alive. Maybe happiness was more a question of appreciating his circumstances, whatever they were, than avoiding unhappiness?

51: The Opposite Of Crying Oneself To Sleep

"We're live from the hospital where the mayor is receiving treatment for depression and burn-out."

The TV-reporter stood in the wind outside the block of concrete that was the city's main hospital. A few months back, the mayor had been accused of embezzlement and corruption, and was under police investigation. Now, he apparently had a nervous breakdown.

"None of the mayor's representatives are currently available for comment," said the reporter.

A blond man in a white chicken suit and yellow legs appeared behind the journalist. While she talked, the giant chicken circled in the background, clucking loudly and flapping his arms. The cameraman moved sideways to get the chicken out of the shot, but the birdman followed, making enthusiastic chicken noises. When the reporter became aware of the prank, she fell quiet. The broadcast blacked out, then went to commercial break.

He began to laugh. He laughed and laughed and couldn't stop. When he thought about the birdman's demonstration of opinion about the mayor's "burn-out", and the reporter's face when she realized what was going on, he started to laugh again. The mirth rose up inside him, he couldn't keep it down. He had bouts of laughter when he went to bed, during the next day, and in the evening when Katsuhiro visited him.

Katsuhiro thought he had gone crazy. When he tried to describe the chicken scene to his brother, who had missed the broadcast, he began to laugh again. He could barely get the words out. Katsuhiro shook his head.

He usually got the laughing fits when he shouldn't laugh, like at school or at work. Trying to suppress them just made it worse, like some kind of laughing Tourette's. Eventually, the words or experiences that led to the laughing fits evaporated from his mind, along with the need to laugh.

Sometimes he had them inside dreams, and laughed so hard he woke from it. Waking up laughing was a strange, but welcome sensation. It was the opposite of crying oneself to sleep.

52: The Measure Of All Things

Nothing in the empty city judged or assessed him. The silence made no demands, expected nothing. It had room for everything he felt and thought and did, and accepted it causelessly. That was no small thing.

The rules were up to him. There were no rules. There were no expectations. He was the measure of all things, whether he deemed them valuable or wasted, good or bad, useful or useless. All human judgment was fleeting in the sea of stars. Quietude, silence and eternity was all there was.

He felt he ought to make a new world, create new and independent ways, new thoughts and emotions and ways of living. But the world didn't need to be saved and certainly not by him, so he left the idea and felt lighter for it.

At night, his bed shook. The mattress and bed vibrated, even when he was lying still. It was strange and eerie. He watched it and let it play out.

53: Culture Shock

In the holidays, when they arrived in their father's country after a whole day's flight from home, their grandmother always served a special welcoming meal.

He usually started with a square piece of silken bean curd that had a small amount of fresh ginger grated on top of it. The strong flavor of the ginger contrasted beautifully with the creaminess of the smooth curd. Each time he bit into the ginger, he was surprised by the flavor. It was a delightful little meal in itself.

Then he picked up the bowl with the main course; a stew made of potatoes, rarely used in any other native dish, but which his grandmother feared they missed from home. The dish also contained beef, carrot, yellow turnip and white turnip that had simmered in stock for a long time. It resembled his mother's stews at home, but the broth was made of foreign ingredients and tasted strangely. The familiar vegetables just made the dish more alien.

He never told his grandmother that, but it must have been clear from his behavior, when he refused a second helping after finishing his bowl before anyone else at the table. And worse, when he didn't even finish the small bowl he was given. Several years in a row he ate less and less of the welcoming stew, out of stubborn, spiteful protest. As he grew older and more considerate, he ate what he received out of courtesy, but it must have disappointed his grandmother that the meals she spent hours preparing were only enjoyed by one of her three grandchildren.

The meal was finished with intensely sweet red bean sauce and grilled rice cakes, a dish usually eaten at the New Year celebration. But his grandmother knew how much they liked the sweet dish and always made it for their arrival.

Finally, there were cookies of sugar and flour pressed into tiny similes of butterflies, dragons, blossoms and carp, taken with hot tea. His grandmother's tea was strong and bitter, but the delicate cookies made it taste sweet and balanced. The memory of those meals was bittersweet.

During the holidays in his father's country, he discovered a liking for the old operatic plays. It surprised his father, as children usually found the deliberate recitation and hymn-like singing tedious. But to him, each sound and instrument stood out more clearly than in the music at home, like the flavors of his

grandmother's meals. He went with his father and grandfather to a few operas. His grandfather's face was somber as always, but his eyes were bright. His father also looked proud, three generations enjoying the same traditional art form together. It was one of the best memories he had of his grandfather, but their quiet joy had been uncomfortable. He couldn't even watch old movies from his father's country without feeling a sting of embarrassment. He could only hope that his own grandchildren would treat him with less ambivalence, if he ever had any
kids.

His brother picked up on his enjoyment for the old operas and teased him mercilessly, called him an old man and a monk. Katsuhiro embraced the popular cultures of both their parents' countries, as well as their nation of residence, shaped his hair into spikes and sang along with vapid pop songs. Katsuhiro studied both languages, organized film evenings at the university and got his first job as a translator of computer games and press kits from publishers in their paternal country. He had always admired Katsuhiro's ability to navigate between three different cultures with ease.

Theresa pretended the issue didn't exist, and as soon as she was old enough to get away from the family trips, she vanished. In the holidays, Theresa went away to pony camps, swim camps and scouting trips, and in her late teens, for hiking and music festivals, with Beanie and their pack of shrieking female friends.

He also attempted to make himself busy in the summer, with photography classes, soccer tournaments, working as a paperboy or as an animal shelter volunteer. But the few times he did manage to get away from the family trips, he felt too guilty to enjoy it.

The stays in their mother's country were no easier than the holidays in the east, even though he learned the language faster than his father's tongue. The food was familiar from his mother's cooking, but the landscape and climate was foreign.

Compared with his father's country, there were fewer traditions, but still subtle codes of behavior. People seemed open and informal, most laughed and spoke loudly. But if he said too much or failed to acknowledge another person's place in the near invisible social hierarchy, he received glances and grins. Being too courteous or formal was even worse, then he was an oddity.

Michael and Beanie were in a similar situation. They visited their mother's country every summer. Once, when they all stayed at their grandparents' house, he tried to share his experiences with Michael. Michael just muttered that the entire country was backwards and stupid, as was the language and culture, and remained sour for the rest of the afternoon.

He walked alone to the stubbly field at the edge of the residential area and fed the small pony that was tied there. The animal looked at him softly while it chewed the grass and rapeseed plants he offered it.

54: Uvular

On the way to his parents' house for Sunday dinner, he drove out to the silica plant south of the city. The factory's hygroscopic beads soaked humidity during shipping and storage. The material also made excellent cat litter. It was cheaper to buy at the plant than in the pet store.

The city's industrial section was worn factories, rusty towers, tall burn pipes and mounds of sand, mud and byproducts. He found the landscape beautifully brutal. Factories and plants cared little for human life. Profit, productivity, industry and work were the valued characteristics in that world. Stories of lives spent in hard labor at starvation wages frightened him more than tales about monsters. Ghosts were intangible, industry was concrete, and sometimes, inescapable.

In the car, he wet a clean handkerchief with water from a bottle he had bought in the city, and held the moist fabric over his nose and mouth. Outside, white silica dust clung to every surface and sprinkled the lot like *ersatz* snow. The dust irritated his eyes and lungs.

A moving band transported gray lumps of sodium silicate between two corrugated towers. Metallic booms, clangs and squeals vibrated in the air. Two employees wheeled a gas tank and metal plates through the enormous doors of the factory building. Both were dressed in coveralls, masks and gloves. He doubted that was enough to keep the dust away.

The foreman's office was a small hut attached to the factory wall. When he entered, the easterner looked up from his phone call and nodded. He returned the nod and sat down by the desk.

The room's faded turquoise walls reminded him of sunny skies when there wasn't fog every day, and blue lagoons on the southern continent. The low space smelled of old cigarette smoke and industrial cleaner.

On the wall behind the foreman, hung a calendar from the previous year, the paper yellowed and the corners bent. An eastern sky goddess in pink, blue and yellow silk, with a red scarf around her shoulders, danced among stylized clouds. The days and dates, printed in bright red ink, hadn't faded at all.

The goddess looked happy. Her pink mouth curled in a secretive smile. Maybe she knew when the sun would burn through the fog and the skies would clear? Maybe never? Perhaps that was the reason for her mirth?

The foreman finished his call and grinned up at him, revealing stained teeth behind creases of dark skin. He shook hands with him while he tried to avoid looking at the bald pate covered with oily, side-parted hair. The foreman wore the same dark coveralls as his employees, but thick shoes instead of boots.

"Another carton of crystals?" the foreman said.

"Yes, thank you."

"I always keep a stack ready for you pet lovers." The small man nodded at some cardboard boxes in the corner. They had no logo and were taped shut.

He smirked and nodded.

"Our snow still bothering you?"

He nodded again.

"But the crystals are good enough for your cats?"

There was an insult there he didn't get, so he remained silent.

"I'm afraid our manufacturing costs have increased," the foreman said. Just like last time.

"How much?" he said and coughed.

The greasy man named a price two percent higher than previously. Was he making fun of him? The cat litter would soon be cheaper to buy in the pet shop, without the long drive and the irritated airways. But he had to get back to the car. He put a note that covered the price plus a little more on the table.

"Keep the rest," he said and pushed the paper across the stained wood.

The foreman picked up the note and placed it in his breast pocket.

"You still think our factory is beautiful?" he said with a knowing tip of the chin.

He suddenly saw the humor in the situation and grinned. "You know I do," he said. "As well as last year's weather goddess."

"I keep her just for you." The foreman laughed loudly. The red uvula at the back of his throat danced like an animal strung up for gutting.

55: Imaginary Hoops

The picture of the dancing weather goddess made him recall that he had once met an eastern goddess in his dreams. As a teenager, he had seen a tall lady in an elaborate red dress with a long train, her black hair piled high, walk stately through his dream. She had two young maidens in flimsy white clothing and floor-length hair at her side. When he approached to look at them, he was fenced off by the attendants.

"Stay, stay away," the maidens sang and whirled their long white sleeves in the air. It was probably meant to look elegant and judicial, but it just made him want to catch the fabric and swing the maidens over his head after their sleeves.

"You are not yet worthy to meet the goddess," the two maidens sang-explained.

He let them push him back and saw the goddess disappear into the crowd of dream people. If the goddess didn't think he was good enough to speak with her, he didn't give a damn about what she had to say or how many imaginary hoops she had jumped to get where she was. Then the dream ended.

Last year he had spotted the goddess again. He recognized her as a dream character he had encountered before, and approached her. That time her maidens danced for him; slow, intricate steps in a beautiful garden lit by traditional stone lanterns. But when he drew closer to the goddess herself, he was once again denied with a melodious:

"Not yet, not yet."

When he woke up, he remembered the earlier dream about the goddess. How long did he keep his dream characters? Once created they lasted forever?

56: Delta

He took the train to the old section of the city and a restaurant he used to visit as a student. The food there had been good, plentiful and inexpensive. Now he longed to re-experience the past.

The grate that protected the door was open and there was light in the windows. The restaurant was still in business.

He descended three steps to the entrance and its two red columns encircled by golden wood dragons. The dust between the dragons' scales, on their curling whiskers and inside their hollow pupils, was just as thick as he remembered it.

He entered to shade and the warm smell of food. To the right was a dark, closet-sized room, filled from floor to ceiling with shelves. The shelves were crammed with brown binders and stacks of yellow paper. Below the shelves sat a thin, pot-bellied man behind a square desk, writing in the light from an old lamp with a flexible metal neck.

Between the tiny office and the red arch to the dining hall, stood an eighty liter aquarium with black and white pebbles on the bottom, no plants. An orange carp swam in the cloudy water. The aquarium made him smile. It used to house black lobsters, their under water fights sounding like castanets. Now there was only the fat fish.

He nodded at the host in the office, and the skinny man nodded back. The host barked a name and a young woman with her hair in a nervous bun appeared. She wore a short, tight-fitting dress with a long split up the side, and a pale smile.

"Follow me," she said softly. She guided him to a seat beneath the small windows that peered out on the street.

"Would you like this table?" she said. Pant legs and shoes flashed by the glass. It was too busy for him.

"I'll sit here," he said and pulled out a chair one row from the windows. The young woman nodded and put a worn plastic folder down on the golden tablecloth.

He ordered what he had enjoyed so many times before; pork fried in oil and batter, served with sugar and rice vinegar sauce, hot, sweet tea for last. He watched the grime in the window sill outside, and the buses and cars that roared by.

In the warm and muted afternoon he ogled the waitress' legs, wishing her dress were even shorter.

57: Deoxyribonucleic acid

He had thought that if he broke the routine of working nine hours a day, five days a week, eleven months a year, his life would disintegrate. Only when he was sick or on holiday did he break the habit. Not being in the routine meant being sick, something he didn't want to be.

But now he realized that even without the routine, there would still be life and he would still be living.

Everything in his life, even his body, was temporary. He would enjoy it for as long as it lasted, but it wasn't really his. Everything belonged to the silence, because everything played out inside it.

If all he did for the rest of his life was feed the cats, eat and sleep, not going anywhere, no career, no so-called life progress, nothing in the silence would blame him.
And, he suspected, it would not change the view at the end of his life much. What was the point of the so-called life progress if it didn't lead anywhere?

58: Meat

He stood on a high cliff above a turquoise lake of melt water from the mountains. The cliff sides were too steep to climb, loose sandstone that would crumble at a touch.

He didn't jump off the edge and fly away as he had done in other dreams. Instead, he attuned himself to the song of the earth of the cliff, the stone and sand, and decreased the frequency in increments. That lowered his position until he stood on the lake surface. The water lapped at his bare feet. It was cold and pure. He closed his eyes and opened his hands.

When he next woke inside the dream, he was a teenage boy sitting on a floor of golden tiles by a large fireplace. The fire was lit and burned high, but the orange flames provided only light, no heat. The rest of the room was in shadows. He wore a white cloth around his waist and narrow bands of gold around his arms and knees.

On the floor between his naked legs lay a human torso. Its eyes and lips and ears had been stitched shut with red twine. He thrust his hand into the torso and pulled out a stiff and sinewy heart. It had stopped beating a long time ago and the fat around it was hard and white. The operation covered his hands in red and yellow.

He gagged, but his dream self felt a deep satisfaction with the work, and continued to clean out the torso in long, flowing motions. He put the organs down in clay bowls on the floor, while he sang softly to himself. When his hands grew too slimy, he cleared them by smearing red script, pictorial characters of the song he was singing, on the tiles.

He screamed. He didn't know what the words meant, but the ritual cleaning and the song frightened him deeply.

"It's just a dream," he told himself. But he couldn't change it, only watch. His young dream-self continued his disgusting work while he sang in the soft, flickering darkness.

He woke feeling sweaty and sick, and pushed the duvet away. The gray cat lifted her head and moved to rest her chin on his upturned wrist. He closed his eyes, exhausted and unsettled. He prayed there wouldn't be an article in the morning's paper about a human torso found emptied of organs in the city.

59: Letting The Horses Run

He couldn't spend all three weeks of his sick leave sleeping and dreaming, even though he wanted to. He needed something to do, something to fill the days with. Because of the splint, he couldn't run or swim or climb as he usually did when he was bored. Even sedentary activities such as walking and reading were painful. But using the camera with tripod worked well.

Thus, he took pictures, with long breaks between each shot to adjust the tripod, focus, aperture and shutter speed with his left hand. He photographed the cats and items in the apartment, and family and friends when they came to visit.

When his hand grew better, he took pictures of the underground garage, the honeycomb towers, the train station and the park. Then he shot buildings, bridges, homes and shops in the area. For a period he used a fish eye lens to make the pictures look spherical and bounded, including self-portraits.

When he tired of that, he photographed the empty city and the waiting stillness, by capturing the space between objects. He tried to make the emptiness shine like it did in his eyes.

Katsuhiro wondered where he got the energy from to photograph all day for days.

"It's no problem," he said, "because I like it so much." The truth was that he had to do it, it had become an obsession. He put the obsession like horses before a cart and let them run as fast and as much as they wanted.

60: A Cure For Consumerism

He went through his belongings; films, books, music, games, clothes, shoes, gadgets, furniture, the little sea of things he had amassed over the years.

Everything he no longer needed or liked, he cleared out in cardboard boxes and plastic bags. The games and gadgets went to Katsuhiro, the films to Michael, the music and books to Beanie, and the rest to recycling.

"You can't throw this out!" Beanie said, holding a CD with a blue cover up to him. "It's a part of music history!"

"Don't worry," he said. "I won't miss it and it won't miss me."

"But I already have a copy," Beanie said.

"Keep two or give it to a friend," he suggested.

He carried the bags to the recycling bins at the train station. But he couldn't hand in clothes and shoes there, so he took the bags back to the garage for disposal.

At the back of the closet he found two designer shirts and a pair of expensive jeans. In his eagerness to gain items and return to the treadmill to earn money for more, he had forgotten his acquisitions almost as soon as he bought them. Was he that addicted to things? Cleaning out and getting rid of what he didn't need, and the knowledge that he now needed fewer things, made him feel light and new.

61: Wandering

The sick leave meant more time in the white emptiness, which felt soft and good. But he also feared the lack of activity, because there was no place to hide from his frustration.

He read about people who knew and worked towards their purpose, or found their calling and went to it, happily leaving their former occupations behind. The stories were supposed to be inspiring, but instead he felt defeated.

Returning to school was not an option, neither was going back to his previous employer. He had to find an alternative, but what?

That night he was back in the canoe, traveling along the dream coast, on his way to the icy wastes in the north. This time he was guiding his sister, who paddled behind him.

He turned to see how Theresa was doing. She was unstable in her canoe and had problems staying afloat in the agitated sea. But she continued on, yelped when a wave almost overturned her, laughed when she tried to catch up with him, digging her paddle furiously into the bright water. He smiled. It felt good to help his sister as they traversed the familiar route along the coast of his dreams.

But he was the one who fell in, and drew his breath sharply before he went under. He knew the icy water would shock the air out of his lungs. A silver light flared up inside him and he vanished.

62: Weakness

He woke up feeling he was about to disappear completely. He opened his eyes and took in the ceiling, lifted his hands into his field of vision. He wasn't there. There was just silent emptiness.

Vanishing like that wasn't new, but now the feeling of nothingness frightened him. It felt like he was at the gates of death. If more of him disappeared, there would be nothing left, not even a body! He sat up and turned the light on, sweating with fear. The horrible sensation was over in a few minutes and he returned to sleep.

But a few days later, he woke inside the fear and the nothingness again. He tried to sit up, but was so tired he couldn't move. He could only tolerate the emptiness and let it cover him.

One humid afternoon it happened when he was awake. He felt sleepy and was overcome with tiredness. Suddenly, he was nothing at all, and had several flashes of white light. He tried to focus on something inside himself, but it was gone, there was nothing there. He was dying! The world faded out of view. He thought he was going to faint, but that didn't happen. He had several more flashes of light. Slowly, the nothingness receded and his mind returned to its previous state.

The fear vanished as if nothing had happened, the rest of the day was quiet. The world didn't care about his supposed brush with death and neither did his thoughts. They came and went as usual. Everything continued like before.

He thought about a film from his father's country, about a group of childhood friends that were separated by the desire a young lover stirred in them. It was years since he had watched the film. He had forgotten most of it, but a few scenes stood out with eidetic clarity in his mind.

His own memories were like that. Some of them he could replay with great accuracy. Other parts he barely recalled and some things were gone. He only heard about them when his family and friends talked about the past.

63: The Doer Of His Deeds

He ate dinner. Every time he leaned forward to put the meat on his fork into his mouth, the light at the back of his mind flared up and swallowed him.

He thought about achievements. None of what he had attained in life could he claim as his own. For most of his life he had thought he was the doer of his actions. But when he thought about photography, how the ideas, angles and shots came to him, instead of from him, he realized that it was the same with all the other things he did. Why take pride in anything? It was inspiration, the silence, that did it all.

But what about acts that intended to harm or kill? How could the silence be so hateful as to inflict suffering and death on another part of itself? Suffering was a subjective experience, but if that was what the individual felt, how could one disregard it?

The day was dry and sunny, with a tall, bright sky. In the evening, clouds gathered and a cold breeze blew in from the ocean. It felt like the summer was coming to the end.

64: Dreaming In A Box

The insomnia returned. He woke staring at the ceiling behind sleeping eyelids, and felt the openness and stillness of the room. At night, falling asleep was a struggle, because he knew how he'd wake up. A small area of his forehead, between and above his eyebrows, darkened to an elongated mark.

From the shore of sleep the room looked like a coffin. His body slept inside it, a stone on the bed. It was like seeing himself dead while he was still alive. It was more disgusting than viewing the stacks of people that slept around him, because now he was the corpse.

Falling into dreamless sleep wasn't any better, because then his mind was elsewhere and he had no knowledge of what happened to his body. He worried about it.

But everything he did and thought took place in the silence. The emptiness was just as peaceful when he slept as when he was awake. He didn't need to be concerned about his body. When he saw that he fell into dreamless sleep with the cats next to him in the open room.

Something soft and warm reached him from the space inside his mind. It was vast and loving. He had felt that warmth for most of his life, but not reflected on it. Now it shone through his thoughts and emotions. It felt like sleeping in the sun, the heat and the light the sun gives to the Earth and all the other planets, shining without intent or selection Was it love?

65: The Present Rather Than The Past

The days passed. He did his best to appreciate the emptiness he lived in and to relax his hold on old hurts.

He slowly let go. Living inside the openness was preferable to anything else, because it felt peaceful.

Doing things just for the money or the status took all the beauty and fun out it. He had to relinquish his fears and focus on what felt good.

It was never up to him anyway. Whether he had a job, or got a job, or earned money, or became poor. There was little difference between him letting go of control and worry, to realizing he was not in control of what happened to him at all. Even the decision to decide, came to him, it did not originate in him. It had always been the silence.

66: Flayed

He dreamed he cut an incision across someone's foot
with a broad blade, peeled the skin back, and kept it on
the cold metal with his thumb. Then he pulled, turning
the small fold of skin into a long strip. He pulled and
pulled, up a leg, across a torso and along an arm. The
skin revealed red striated muscle and white sinews and
joints. It was like preparing a tender and exotic steak.

Carefully, he repeated the process: cut a shallow
incision and peeled, like a chef creating a fine meal.
Despite the subject matter, he was calm. He felt no fear
or disgust, just surprise at his observations. Then he
realized what he was doing. He was flaying a human
being.

He blinked. He was skinning something or someone,
uncovering layer after layer. He had a feeling it was
himself. That must be it, the right interpretation of the
dream. But even after that realization, he remained calm
and relaxed. He sank back into blank sleep.

Afterwards, he dreamed of tall mountains with glittering
snow, where lines of colored flags whipped in the
booming wind. He sat on a crumbled wall above a cold
lake, herding black crows.

67: Fireworks For Adults

The landmine detonated in a plume of asphalt, dirt and sand. The explosion rose three meters in the air, then collapsed into a lose mound, impotent earth once more. It was fireworks for adults.

"Good job, Minesweeper," Kepler said on the radio.

He smirked at the nickname.

In the beginning he shot mostly landmines, picked them off roads and paths under direction of the mine crews. It felt good to make life for the convoys and patrols easier. But his tasks turned increasingly pre-emptive.

He crouched on top of the stairs, behind the banister, so he could watch the staircase below and the office across the street without being seen. He was friends with buildings, navigated them with ease and rarely got lost in them.

He felt the attackers before he saw them. Their breathing, shallow and uncertain, betrayed them. They rushed up the stairs, hoping speed was enough for a successful ambush. He rose and shot the first. The high powered round disintegrated a hand held up to shield, then exploded in the man's chest. The body tumbled back into the emptiness of the stairwell, turned over and over, as if it fell from a great height.

Mortensen got the other with a small weapon, its two shouts so close to his head that his ears sang. He scanned the staircase for more ambushers, nothing. He breathed. He had thought a close range kill would look monumental, but there had only been helplessness in the other man's eyes. The body landed at the bottom of the stairs, crumpled and discarded like dirty underwear.

"We owned them!" Mortensen yelled behind him. "Yeah, Minesweeper!"

A surprisingly large amount of people had survived the air raid. A surprisingly large amount of them were youths and children, some armed, some not. The helicopters banked, their hard hail kicking up sand and soil. The enemy scattered and ran towards his placement above them.

"They're coming your way," Kepler said in his ear. "Get ready, Minesweeper."

He exhaled softly and refined the aim, wishing he could go back to shooting mines.

68: Leaving The Universe

There were so many things to watch in the rioting crowd, to keep under control. He slid the scope from body to body, but couldn't make out anyone clearly. It was an amorphous mass of arms and heads and mouths that shouted and moved and punched the air. Their anger hit him in the belly. Inside the gloves, his hands were slick and cold.

Something like a grenade flew in an arc towards him. It hit the edge of the vehicle and bounced off the metal. It was a stone. Someone in the crowd laughed. He swung the barrel, wasn't going to shoot without clearance, just scare them a little, just...

He was not there, not in the picture anymore. The afternoon sky was orange, the emaciated trees in the distance were dry and brown, the buildings decrepit and dirty, the street dusty, the crowd roared in anger. The stock was hard against a shoulder, the edge of the vehicle ended in empty air. But there was no him who saw that, heard those sounds and ceased his breath for the shot. All those things happened, but they shone alone.

He was not there, he was no one, a no-thing, yet awake and moving. He fell down into the interior of the vehicle, burning with nothingness.

He asked for a medical discharge. Kepler tried to persuade him to remain, and became annoyed when he didn't change his mind. Painful emotions radiated from the officer like gamma particles. Being around him hurt. He saluted Kepler and left.

"Always so damn stubborn," Kepler said to his back.

He ran for the bus to the airport before Mortensen could find him. Standing in the warm terminal, he realized he had to see the ocean. Instead of boarding the plane home, he exited the building and continued down the road in the direction of the coast.

69: A Catalyst For Silence

He knew he should have gone home, but something had started up in him, something he couldn't stop. Instead, he went to the Coast of Bones, carrying only the clothes he was wearing. The desert accepted him as one of its own, promised to eat his bones too, if it defeated him. He was grateful for that.

Finally, he found himself in an unknown southern country. There he was arrested for vagrancy. The embassy repatriated him grudgingly. Because he was listed as missing, they had to pay for his flight home. In the city, his father refused to talk to him.

"Yuki, father was convinced you were dead, or you'd let us know where you were," Katsuhiro said softly in their paternal language. "He wanted to arrange a burial rite for you, but mom stopped him."

"I'm sorry," he replied in the same tongue.

"Why didn't you come home?" Katsuhiro's eyes flitted over his face to read his intent, his past, his reason.

"I'm not sure," he said in the language of the city. "I wanted to see the ocean."

"How was it?" Katsuhiro said in the same tongue as before.

"It didn't look like I thought it would."

"And that's why you came home?"

"Of course not," he said. "I wanted to see you."

"Don't exert yourself," Katsuhiro finished.

When a friend of the family told him there was an entry level position available, prior experience an advantage but not essential, he applied for the job. There was no more room for mistakes.

It had been a catalyst for silence. But now he could let it go, because it had long since let go of him. There was a great freedom and relief in that knowledge.

70: Freedom Is Accepting That You Are Free

For a long time he had equated himself with his mind. He thought he was a mind located somewhere inside his head. But the summer's close examination of the sensory experience had revealed that he, the center of awareness, wasn't inside his head. He had never seen the inside of his own head, except for in medical scans.

He wasn't inside his body either. He could sense his body and control it, but it moved across the room, had breakfast, swam in the pool, ran on concrete, healed after surgery, with minimal instructions from him. The body performed its chores, while he daydreamed about eternity.

Instead, he was a point of attention that hovered a little above his body. All objects were present, without there being anyone who saw them or described them. He was slowly getting used to that nothingness.

He felt like a small pocket of individual mind that was closed from the rest of the world with just a single fold. The fold wouldn't be enough to keep the world out in the long run. What would happen when the pouch opened and let the universe into itself? Would it be like a dam bursting or a leaf falling to the ground?

71: The Big Crunch Theory

That night he had one of his disaster dreams. They usually entailed jets crashing down or asteroids hitting the Earth. Other times he had a bizarre dream where the solar system filled with rock, as if the theorized Big Crunch, the end of the cosmological life cycle, were about to start.

It was time for the Big Crunch again. The space between the Earth and the Moon filled up with enormous amounts of stone that materialized from empty vacuum, until the molten rock covered the sky. He could see the stone accumulate all the way out to Saturn. The rocks glowed with lava, but he felt no heat. If the stone filled the solar system, there wouldn't be room for anything else.

"The solar system is filling up with rock, because the universe is ending," he told himself. It felt terrible that the universe was about to end.

But then he realized it was a dream and became very relieved. He also remembered that he had had the dream many times before. It remained in his dreaming memory, the part of his recollection that he could only access from dreams, and which closed when he woke up. He remembered that he had the dream about once a year.

72: Into The White

He spent the rest of the weekend worrying about work, money and the future. On Sunday night he turned off the TV and sat in silence.

The concern and emotions receded and the open and empty world came into view. Without the weight of the troubled thoughts and emotions, his body relaxed and his head cleared. It was like taking a vacation from the worries. He knew what he had to do. He had resisted the idea, like the trip to the tunnels and the tuberculosis hospital, but no more.

On Monday morning, he handed in his resignation at work. Carla was disappointed, but not surprised.

"You have been brooding for months, so I knew you were unhappy," she said. "I called your report folder "Black Hen Files". Look." She pointed at an icon on her laptop screen.

They laughed together. It sounded like one voice. He no longer owed her anything.

"I'm sorry," he said. "I know I haven't made your life easy."

"You did what I told you to do, most of the time," Carla said and smiled.

He smiled back at her.

"So what are you going to do now?" Carla said.

"I don't know," he said. "Nothing, I think, for a while."

"You'll be fine," Carla said and hugged him. "I know it. Good luck."

When it was done, he felt only relief. It felt like he had saved himself months of frustration. The relief surprised him. Had he been that scared of letting go? Now he intended to do what felt meaningful. He needed a vocation, a calling.

Two days later, a former colleague, who had returned to university to complete an advanced degree after years of working, told him that the institute needed a photographer to shoot images of owls in auditory experiments, document an upcoming dissection of a giant squid, and clean and scan a storage room's worth of old microscope slides. There were good chances for more work later on. He had no fear of birds of prey, or tentacles, and immediately accepted the job.

73: The Crabs

As soon as the cumbersome splint and elastic bandage was exchanged for a less restricting brace and buddy-taping of his fingers, he started driving to get out of the apartment and away from the cabin fever.

The ocean road curved south along the bay, past the unattractive concrete silos, hunched-over factory buildings and old wooden docks of the feed plant. Its slim burn chimneys exhaled the stench of rotten fish and death from unnamable interior processes in invisible, but undeniable clouds of flatulence.

On bad days not even the honeycomb towers on the other side of the marsh were exempt from the olfactory assault. The plant's owners had received so many complaints about its looks and odors from the public, press and politicians, that they finally hid it from view with a tall wooden fence. That helped against the sight but did nothing for the smell.

It had been a clear day, one of the few that summer. A collapsed stretch of the feed plant fence showed the orange sun slipping towards the horizon.

There was something on the road. At first he thought it was a spill on the asphalt, but when he drove closer he saw that the road was living, moving. Thousands, no tens of thousands, of crabs with purple-reddish shells and yellow feet moved across the road in an unexpected crustacean exodus. Were they fleeing the pollution in the bay?

He stopped the car. The migrating crabs tumbled over each other through the gap in the fence, and surged into the ditch between the beach and the road. From there, the stream of hard-shelled bodies flowed across the asphalt, over the shoulder on the other side and into the dry dunes, where tall, sharp-edged grass shivered in the evening breeze.

At first he wanted to go out and fill the back seat with crabs. Maybe they were good to eat? But then he remembered where the crustaceans came from. They were probably full of heavy metals and carcinogens. Best to take the inland road home tonight. He shifted the gear stick gently with his wounded hand and started backing.

The sound of breaking crab shells was audible even over the song of the engine. The rear-view mirror told him he had gone too close to the crabs. Now they were filling up the road behind him as well as in front. Perhaps he could navigate around them? Or if he drove slowly enough, their shells wouldn't blow the tires? He aimed for the middle of the road, away from the crab-filled ditches, and moved the car carefully.

There was a series of loud cracks. One tire went and then another. Great. The salty body-fluid smell of crab juice drifted into the car. He had no choice but to abandon ship. He got out, the car dinged in protest of the open door. He kicked the noisy thing shut. Paradoxically, the stink from the feed plant was weaker here than further away and downwind.

What should he do? Phone Katsuhiro for transport home? Call a taxi? He wondered what the insurance claim would sound like. He was almost looking forward to writing it.

The crabs spilled over his shoes, pant legs and ankles. They pushed and jostled and crawled over each other in several layers, many scuttling fast, some walking leisurely, others weaving confusedly, but all moving in the same direction, as if they were a single mind. To the crabs he didn't even exist. He was just another obstacle, a part of the warm road and the sand and the grass they had to cross on their way inland.

He sat down on the car's silver-colored hood and looked at his body and the background of moving crabs. They were all inside his perception. His body was just closer in space than the bodies of the crabs.

From that perspective, his body and the crabs were the same, simply objects, the same as all the other objects in his field of vision; the fence, the beach, the setting sun.

While he watched, his thoughts and emotions flitted by, uninterrupted and untouched by the movements of his body and the crustaceans. His mental activity and the bodies were all inside a soft, but alive awareness that encompassed the car and the beach and the fence and everything else. The consciousness was gigantic, it filled the world. The city was both empty and full, of a warm and living presence.

He watched the glowing awareness and the bodies in his field of vision intensely. When the sun was obscured completely by the ocean, he waded through the crabs, and walked home to the honeycomb towers in the warm and cicada-filled darkness.

74: A Landscape Of Absolute Peace

He sat in the sofa with his laptop, writing the insurance claim for the car, when an image blossomed up inside him.

He looked out over a small lake between round mountains. It was dusk and the sun had just fallen behind the summits. The sky glowed deep red. The water on the lake was still, and the air was soft and warm. There were no sounds, not even of dusk-active insects or animals.

The landscape was silent. There was no sense of wilderness or desolation or lack of any kind. Time had vanished. It was a landscape of absolute peace. It was deeply beautiful and restful.

He lifted his head in wonderment and was back in the living room. He closed his eyes. Even the memory of the image filled him with peace. He could feel the warmth, the soft air against his skin and the mild dusk light behind his eyes.

75: **Returning**

When he opened his eyes again, his sense of being a mind and a body separate from the rest of the world, was gone.

He had believed he was a single body in a world full of objects and others. But now he saw that everything he perceived existed inside the bright, loving awareness he had seen on the night of the crabs. The enormous awareness filled the world like a soft ocean, surrounded and embodied him and everything else; the sofa, the TV, the living room, the apartment, the tower, the city, the planet, the universe itself. And it was him, he was that ocean, that awareness, that beingness.

It was nothing new. He was not his body, thoughts, emotions or actions, no matter how hurt, convincing or questionable they were. He had never been confined inside a body or been a disembodied spirit, he had just been more aware of his body, emotions and thoughts than the rest of himself. When he had become aware of his own awareness, and sensed the act of sensing, it had looked like white flashes.

The gap between his thoughts, the space between his in-breath and out-breath, had widened to include the entire world, the cosmos. He was the living, warm awareness which all thoughts and emotions and actions took place inside. He was the vast and loving consciousness and being, and it was him.

In that limitless awareness, problems, sadness, regret, or any other constriction, turned tiny and powerless. His past dissolved like ice in water, there was nothing more to do, no denial or story or absolution. It was only life; shining, flowing and ebbing as it wanted, unhindered, free and open.

Now the world played out inside him, instead of him being in the world somewhere. He was completely and irrevocably real.

76: Early Fall

A cold wind blew in from the north. The temperature sank and the sky turned tall and gray, with large clouds that rushed to the horizon.

After three months of humidity and heat, the lower temperature was welcome, even if it was cold for early August. It felt like a release, a benediction.

On the balcony, the garden chairs stood unfolded. They were open to the sky and the wind.

It started to rain. The drops were cold and clear, the size of almonds. They floated down as slowly and gently as snow, as methane on Titan, and landed without a sound.

He stood on the blotched concrete and smiled into the rain.